A I

M000196312

By Elizabeth Kelly

Chapter 1

"You embarrassed me tonight."

She sighed. "What did I do this time, Barry?"

He frowned at her. "Don't smart mouth me, Lily. You know I hate it when you smart mouth me."

She pressed her lips together and stared out the windshield at the darkness and the rain. "Sorry."

"You always are." He replied.

"Tell me how I embarrassed you." She didn't look at him. "I hardly said a word."

"That's my point, Lily. How do you think it makes me look to have my wife standing there like an uneducated lump in front of my boss? Christ, you're home all goddamn day – you can't turn the TV on and get caught up on current events?"

She stayed silent. It did no good to argue when he was in this type of mood. She knew perfectly well that she could be sitting here being chastised like a small child for speaking too much at the office party. With Barry you never knew what was going to set him off.

The wipers made a thin squealing noise as they swiped across the windshield and Barry cursed under his breath. "Goddammit. I paid forty thousand dollars for this car. You'd think it would have better goddamn wipers."

The rain poured down and Lily cleared her throat nervously. "You should slow down, Barry. It's been raining all evening and the roads are wet."

"Shut up, Lily." Barry said with exasperation. He glanced over and looked her up and down. "What have you been eating lately? That dress barely fits you now. I won't have a fat wife. Do you hear me?"

"Yes. I hear you." She replied softly. She rested her hand briefly on the round curve of her belly. The evening had started out promising. Barry had been in a good mood when he got home from work and he had been excited about the party. She knew he was angling for a promotion and his new boss, Fred Gibson, seemed to think her husband was the bees' knees.

"If I get this promotion, babe," Barry had said as they dressed for the party, "we'll never have to worry about money again."

Lily had smiled encouragingly, although secretly she wondered why they needed more money. They were wealthy, very wealthy at least by her standards, and she thought it was stupid of Barry to constantly be comparing them to their friends. She continued to rub the gentle swell of her belly as a small, bitter smile crossed her face. They were no more her friends than the money was hers.

"You're going on a diet, starting tomorrow." Barry suddenly barked. "Jesus, we've been married seven years and you're already starting to let yourself go? My father warned me this would happen."

She shook her head. "Barry, I'm not getting fat."

"It's probably your cooking. Do you know how to cook anything that isn't swimming in butter and oil?"

"Barry, I'm not getting fat." She repeated.

He ignored her and she sighed and nodded off and on as he began his tirade of abuse. She stared blankly out the windshield. A month ago, when she had stared at the small pink plus sign on the pregnancy test she had, for the first time, acknowledged to herself that something needed to change.

Barry had provided for her, had taken care of her after her parents died and she had been left floundering like a fish out of water, but that didn't mean he was good for her. A man didn't need to use his fists to be abusive. Barry may have never hit her but after years of emotional and mental abuse, she had a hard time not believing the things he said about her. Did she want their child to witness the way he berated her? Or worse – what if he spoke to their child the way he spoke to her?

She made a sudden, rash decision as Barry snorted impatiently. "Are you listening to me, Lily?"

"No."

"You know, the – "

He stopped and looked at her, his mouth dropping open. "What did you just say?"

She took a deep breath, filling her lungs with the smell of his aftershave, before clasping her hands together tightly in her lap. "I said no, I wasn't listening to you. It's all the same shit coming out of your mouth and I'm tired of hearing it."

"Nice mouth on you!" He snapped at her. "Christ! Maybe you could try being like Mr. Gibson's wife. She's a real classy lady. I bet you'd never hear her cursing like a common whore."

Her stomach was rolling and churning with nausea and her hands were ice cold but she made herself continue. "I want a divorce, Barry."

"What?" He gasped.

"I want a divorce. I'm done with you and your abuse."

"Abuse? You silly little twit! When have I ever fucking laid a hand on you? I've treated you like a queen for our entire marriage!" Barry shouted.

"I don't care. I'm leaving you."

"And where are you going to go? Huh? You have no money, you're too stupid to get a job and you have no family or friends. You need me, Lily." Barry spat at her.

She could feel herself weakening. He was right. He was always right. Her sudden burst of independence was fading and she clung to it with a grim determination. She had to think about the baby. The baby that she had been so surprised to discover growing inside of her. In the last two years, Barry had rarely touched her. She suspected that he was sleeping around on her. His shirts smelled of cheap perfume and there were too many unexplained late nights.

She hadn't needed a calendar to know that she had become pregnant the night of her birthday. Barry had been unexpectedly sweet to her that day, surprising her with flowers and taking her out for dinner. They had drunk too much wine and later, when they had gone to bed, the combination of the wine and Barry's sweetness had brought on a genuine enjoyment for his touch for the first time in a very long time.

Barry, his hands gripping the steering wheel tightly, glared at her again. "I will never give you up, Lily. Do you hear me? Our marriage ends when, and only when, I say it does. Do you get that? Or are you too goddamn stupid to even – "

"Barry!" Lily screamed. "Watch out!"

She threw her hands up to shield her face as Barry shouted in surprise. He jerked the steering wheel to the right in a last minute attempt to avoid the car that had swerved into their lane. Their front bumpers kissed with an unearthly squealing sound and Lily screamed again as the car rolled twice. Her seat belt locked painfully across her chest and the air bag burst with a muffled thump.

Glass shattered and metal squealed and she gave a thin, wavering shriek as there was a sudden crushing pain in her leg. The car landed right side up in the ditch with a teeth-jarring thud. Her head snapped back like a flower on a stalk and she moaned as the cold rain splashed against her face. The windshield had shattered, showering her with small jagged pieces of glass, and she could feel blood trickling down the side of her head.

Her ears ringing, she lifted one shaking hand to her head and touched it gingerly. Her fingers came away bloody and she stared at them disinterestedly before looking down at her lap. The front of the car had crumpled and she felt a moment of bright panic when she tried to move her legs and realized they were trapped in the twisted metal.

"Barry," she moaned, "I can't get out. I'm trapped. Barry, please..."

The words died in her throat as she turned her head to the left. Barry's head was turned toward her and she made a choked, gasping moan at the emptiness in his light, blue eyes.

"Barry?" She whispered. "Barry?"

Dimly she could hear people shouting, and Barry's horrifyingly empty eyes were lit up by the bright splash of car headlights. She moaned and tried to move her left leg. It sent an agonizing bolt of pain up her entire body and she screamed hoarsely before falling unconscious.

* * *

"Ma'am? Ma'am, can you hear me?"

Lily groaned and tried to lift her hand to her head. Her head was throbbing and her legs were hurting and she was so cold. She screamed thinly when her hand was swallowed in a large, firm grip and her eyes flew open.

"Please! Help me! Please!" She gasped at the bear of a man who was leaning over her.

"You're alright, ma'am. Just stay still, alright?"

She tried to turn her head to look at Barry but there was something around her neck and she couldn't twist her head.

"Don't do that. Try not to move." The man leaning over her said soothingly. He had a deep voice, warm and raspy, and she clung to his hand and gave him a wide-eyed look of panic.

"My legs! I can't feel my legs!"

"It's alright. Your legs are trapped by the car but we're going to get you out of this car in just a few minutes. I promise. What's your name, sweetheart?"

"Lily." She whispered.

"Lily. Like the flower?"

"Yes." She stared into his warm brown eyes and squeezed his hand tightly.

"Well, Lily like the flower, my name is Logan. I'm a firefighter and we're here to help you. Okay?"

"O-okay." Her teeth were chattering with the cold and Logan frowned before starting to lean back.

"Don't leave me!" Her voice was bright with panic.

He squeezed her hand. "I'm not going anywhere, Lily. I promise."

"Rob! Bring me a blanket!" He turned his head and shouted out the broken windshield before turning back to her. "The paramedics are going to be here really soon. We'll get you to the hospital and they'll fix you up."

He smiled down at her and she studied the short, dark beard on his face. "Logan?"

"Yeah?"

"My husband." She tried again to turn her head and he rested his free hand against the side of her head.

"Don't move your head, Lily. We have your neck and head stabilized and it's better if you don't move it until the doctor can check you for spinal injuries."

"Alright." She whispered. "My husband. Is he – "

"Don't worry about anything but staying completely still." He interrupted her. She moaned at the look in his dark brown eyes and tears slipped down her cheeks.

"He's dead, isn't he?" She whispered.

"Lily, don't – "

"Tell me!" She cried. "Is he dead?"

Logan stared down at the small dark-haired woman. Blood was trickling down her face in a steady stream and he could see the dark bruising already beginning to rise on her pale face. Her eyes were a dark blue and her pupils were large in the dim light. She stared up at him pleadingly and he squeezed her hand tightly.

"Yes, he's dead. I'm sorry, Lily."

He blinked in surprise. In the faint light it almost seemed like there was a look of relief on the small woman's face. He blinked again and it was gone. In its place was sorrow and he watched as tears began to course down her face.

"Oh God." She moaned quietly.

"I'm sorry." He brushed back a strand of her dark hair that was caught on her mouth. "I'm so sorry, Lily."

"Please get me out of here." She whispered.

"We will. We're working on it right now." He said soothingly. "Just stay calm and try not to move."

A man appeared, he was short but broad, and he gave Lily a reassuring smile before handing a blanket to Logan. He disappeared into the darkness as Logan covered her with the blanket. She smiled weakly at him and he stroked her hair again.

"I'm so scared."

"I know, sweetheart. It'll be okay." He glanced out the broken windshield. "The paramedics are here. They're going to – "

He was interrupted by Lily's loud gasp. "Logan! I – I can't breathe. My chest – it hurts and I – I can't breathe. Help me!"

Lily clutched at his hand frantically as she began to gasp for air. "Logan, don't leave me! Don't – "

There was another sharp stabbing pain in her chest and she yelped loudly before her eyes rolled up in her head and she slipped into unconsciousness once more.

Chapter 2

"Hello Shawn."

"Hello Lily. How are you doing?"

"I buried my husband two days ago. How do you think I'm doing?"

The small, portly man winced before approaching her. He stared out the window at the rain. "I'm sorry, Lily. I know Barry's will must have come as a shock to you."

"Not really." She shrugged. "Barry was an asshole to me when he was alive. I'm not surprised he's an asshole in death, as well. I guess as his lawyer you didn't really see that side of him, did you?"

The man winced again, his face turning a bright red, and Lily almost felt sorry for him.

"Well um," he cleared his throat nervously, "as Barry's will indicated, he's left everything to his parents. That includes all of his investments, the funds in his personal account, and this house along with all of its contents."

"Yes, I remember." She said softly.

"Given your delicate condition, Mr. and Mrs. Castro are willing to let you stay in the house until after the baby is born."

"That's generous of them."

"They – they've asked me to speak with you about well, about – "

"Just spit it out, Shawn." Lily said wearily.

"They want the baby. They're willing to offer you a hundred thousand dollars if you give up all rights to the baby and allow them to adopt it."

For the first time since he joined her in the room, Lily's gaze fell on him. "They want to buy my baby."

"They want to give it a good life. Barry's parents are financially secure and they'll be able to give their grandchild the life it deserves."

"They don't believe I can do that?" Lily asked softly.

Shawn sighed. "Lily, you have no job, no family and no money."

"Thanks to their son." She said bitterly.

"If I were you, I'd consider their offer." Shawn said hesitantly. "No one is going to hire you with the minimal work experience you have. Babies are expensive. How will you provide for it? You're still young. With this money you can start over, you can have another – "

"Don't you dare say it, Shawn." Lily snapped. "Don't you dare say I can have another child."

The man flushed again. "I'm sorry, Lily."

She stared impassively at him before returning her gaze to the window. "I should never have told them about the baby." She muttered almost to herself.

"You don't have to make your decision right away. Mr. and Mrs. Castro understand this is a hard decision and they're willing to give you a few months to think it over. You can stay in the house, and they're also offering to give you a small portion of Barry's money to keep you afloat while you consider their offer."

"How kind of them." Lily said quietly.

"Just – just consider it, alright?" Shawn patted her hand almost timidly. "You have very few options."

"Go away, Shawn." Lily said wearily as she turned and, gripping the walker firmly in her hands, shuffled carefully towards the doorway. "I'm tired and I need to rest. I trust you can show yourself out."

* * *

Three months later

"Excuse me?"

Rob glanced up from the front seat of the fire truck. A woman, small and dressed in a thick winter jacket, was standing nervously in front of the truck. She had a pink knitted cap on her head and she was holding what looked to be a tray of chocolate chip cookies in her mitten-covered hands.

"Can I help you?" He jumped down and wiped his hands on the seat of his pants. He cocked his head. The woman looked vaguely familiar to him and he studied her carefully as her cheeks, already red from the cold, flushed even brighter.

"My name is Lily. Lily Castro? A few months ago I was in a car accident and you were one of…"

She trailed off, swallowing nervously and Rob gave her a broad grin.

"Right! I remember you. How are you, Ms. Castro? How's your leg?"

"Uh, it's okay. I still limp but I stopped using the cane over a month ago."

"Good, I'm glad to hear it."

She gave him another nervous smile. "Anyway, it occurred to me last week that I had never said thank you for saving my life. I feel terrible about that so I thought I would come by and say, you know, thank you."

"You're welcome." Rob smiled again at her before his eyes dropped to the tray in her hands.

"Oh, I uh, I made you guys cookies. To, you know, say thank you." She flushed. "It seemed like a good idea at the time but now I'm realizing how lame it is. Hey, you saved my life – here, have a cookie."

Rob burst out laughing before reaching out and taking the tray of cookies from her. "Thank you, Ms. Castro. It's actually a great idea. We love cookies."

She blushed and licked her lips nervously. "There was another man. I think his name was Logan? He stayed with me when I was trapped in the car. Is he, uh, working today?"

Rob nodded. "He is. I think he's in the kitchen. Come on back with me."

* * *

"You're shitting me!" Andy's mouth dropped open and he stared in disbelief at Logan.

"I'm not."

"She just fucking crawled into your bed in the middle of the night?"

"Yes. Naked as a jaybird." Logan sighed.

"Jesus Christ." Andy ran a hand through his short blonde hair. "What the fuck, man? Why does that shit never happen to me?"

Logan scratched at his beard. "I didn't want her crawling into my bed naked, Andy. She's supposed to be a nanny for Hazel, not a bed warmer for me."

"Yeah but man, when a woman crawls naked into your bed, you gotta take advantage of that."

"No, I don't." Logan said shortly. "My priority is Hazel, not getting laid."

Andy rolled his eyes. "Being a single dad doesn't mean that you can never have sex again, dude."

Logan snorted. "Thanks for the tip."

"So, what did you do?"

"What do you mean, what did I do? I kicked her out of my bed and told her that her services as a nanny were no longer required."

"Who's with Hazel?" Andy asked.

"Betty's looking after her again for me. The poor woman just wants to retire and spend time with her grandchildren, and I keep dragging her back into my life and my problems."

He scratched again at his beard. "Now I've got to put an ad in the paper again, and try and find someone else who isn't a goddamn sex maniac to look after my kid."

Andy laughed. "I wouldn't mind having a sex maniac living in my house. In fact it's been months since I've fucked – "

"Hey, we got company. Watch your mouth, Andy." Rob said sternly.

Logan and Andy swung around to see Rob standing behind them, a tray of cookies in his hands, and a slender woman in a pink knitted cap standing beside him.

"Hello." She smiled at them nervously and Andy gave her a look of delight.

"Why, hello there."

"Knock it off, Andy." Logan shook his head and stepped toward the woman.

"Hi." He held his hand out and the woman hesitated before stripping off her mittens and allowing her tiny hand to be swallowed by his large one.

"Hi, my name is – "

"Lily. Like the flower." He smiled at her.

"You remember me." She said softly.

"I do. How are you feeling?"

"Good. Kept my leg so, you know, that's pretty good. They thought they might have to amputate it."

He stared down at her left leg as she cleared her throat. "I came to say thank you for saving my life, Mr...?"

"Anderson. Logan Anderson."

"I'm sorry it took me so long to come by. It's been um, a bit of a difficult time."

"That's alright. I understand."

She glanced at the cookies in Rob's hands. "I made chocolate chip cookies. To say thanks."

"That's kind of you. We love cookies around here." Logan smiled at her as Rob unwrapped the cookies and bit into one before handing the tray to Andy.

"God, these are delicious." He said. "Seriously, Ms. Castro. It could be the best cookie I've ever eaten."

Logan watched with amusement as the small woman blushed again. "I like to bake."

She turned back to Logan and after a moment Rob nudged Andy. It was obvious the woman wanted to speak with Logan alone, and Rob grabbed another cookie before tipping his head at the doorway of the kitchen.

"Let's go."

Andy nodded agreeably and the two men left as Lily gave Logan a small smile. "Thank you so much, Mr. Anderson. I – it meant a lot to me that you stayed with me while I was trapped in the car."

"You're welcome, Lily." His voice was as deep and raspy as she remembered and she gazed at his dark beard for a moment before her eyes dropped to his body.

He was wearing loose track pants and a dark blue t-shirt that clung to his upper body. He was obviously in incredible shape, his job would demand it, and her eyes lingered on his biceps before she stared at the broad line of his shoulders.

She flushed when she realized he was watching her stare at him and she took a step backwards. "Anyway, I just really wanted to say thank you again and to let you know that I was um, doing okay."

"I'm really glad. Thank you for dropping by, Lily." He smiled again at her.

"Right. Okay, well I'll um, see you around." She said weakly.

"You bet. Take care of yourself." He watched as she turned away and limped toward the door.

She hesitated and turned back. "Mr. Anderson?"

"Yes?"

"I overheard your conversation with your friend and I was wondering if I could maybe um, apply for the nanny position?"

He blinked in surprise. "Oh, uh – do you have experience with children?"

"I babysat a lot when I was younger and I'm very good with children." She said eagerly as she walked back to him. "You have a daughter, is that right?"

"Yes, Hazel. She's four."

She smiled. "That's a good age."

"It is." He glanced at his watch. "I'm sorry. I actually have to leave soon."

"Oh, of course. I'm so sorry." She gave him a hopeful look. "Could I – that is – would you mind if I applied for the position?"

He studied her for a moment as she twisted her mittens nervously in her hands, before shaking his head. "I don't mind. I'll give you my address. Why don't you drop by this weekend? We can do the interview and you can meet Hazel."

"Great!" She said eagerly. "I would love to meet her."

He wrote his address down on a slip of paper. She took it and then held out her hand. "Thank you again. I'll see you on Saturday then?"

He nodded and shook her hand firmly. "Yes. Say around eleven?"

"Absolutely. Thank you again, Mr. Anderson."

Chapter 3

"Hazel? There's a nice lady coming today to meet you. She might be your new nanny. Would you like that?" Logan asked as he carefully combed the tangles from Hazel's fine, blonde hair.

The little girl didn't reply and Logan sighed softly. It had been nearly six months since her mother died and the little girl hadn't spoken a word since. He missed her sweet voice.

He made himself smile at the little girl as he leaned around her to look at her. "Do you want pancakes for breakfast, baby bug?"

Hazel, her eyes as dark as his, stared silently at him before giving a brief nod.

"Alright. I'll even put chocolate chips in one of them. What do you think about that?" He tickled her lightly and the little girl squirmed off of the bed and left the room without looking at him.

He sighed again and stared out the window at the snow that was falling steadily down. He took Hazel to a therapist twice a week, had been for the last six months, but the woman hadn't made any progress with her. Physically there was nothing wrong with her but emotionally....

He rubbed at the beard on his face before leaving his bedroom. Hazel just needed more time, he told himself grimly. She would be fine. Obviously what she saw was traumatic and it would just take time for her to recover. At least that's what the therapist kept telling him. He just needed to be more patient and not push her to talk before she was ready.

* * *

Lily took a deep breath, straightened her coat and reached for the doorbell. Before she could ring it, the door opened and a little girl stared up at her. She had long blonde hair and dark brown eyes and she was holding a dirty and stained fabric doll. The doll had a ripped pink dress on, only one button eye and most of the yarn that made up her hair was missing. The few strands that were left flapped limply against the doll's head.

Lily crouched down on the cold step and smiled at the little girl. "Hello. You must be Hazel. My name is Lily." She held her hand out but the little girl just clutched her doll more tightly against her bright orange t-shirt and stared silently at her.

"I like your doll." Lily said encouragingly. "What's her name?"

Hazel just stared at her and Lily swallowed nervously. "Is your daddy home, honey?"

"Hazel? Why are you – "

Logan came striding into the hallway and stopped in surprise when he saw Lily crouched in the doorway.

"Hi! You're early." He glanced at his watch.

Lily flushed as she stood up. "Yes, I'm sorry. I can um, I can wait outside until eleven."

"Don't be silly. Come in." He picked up Hazel, kissing her affectionately on the cheek and motioned for Lily to follow him down the hallway.

She slipped her boots off, placing her mittens and hat neatly on top of them, but left her coat on as she followed him down the narrow hallway to the first doorway on the right. It opened up into the living room and she studied it carefully as Logan tossed Hazel into the air before kissing her cheek again and setting her gently on the ground.

The little girl didn't smile or giggle at her father. Instead, still clutching her doll, she moved to the far side of the room where a child-sized, brightly-coloured table with matching chairs was set up. Without looking at either of them, she sat down and, picking up a crayon, lifted a colouring book from the stack that was sitting on the floor and began to colour.

Logan moved a large pile of laundry from one end of the couch, transferring it to the wingback chair that was beside it. The chair was already filled with laundry and she eyed it carefully, wondering if the pile of clothes would simply tip over and bury her when she sat on the couch.

Logan cleared his throat. "Sorry, the place is a bit messy. It's been a couple of weeks since the last nanny and uh, I'm not the greatest housekeeper."

Lily glanced around the room. The room was cluttered and messy but not really dirty, she decided. Children's books lined the short bookshelf on the wall next to the fireplace and toys were scattered across the floor. Pictures, coloured with the shaky hand of a child, were tacked to a bulletin board and there was a plate of half-eaten pancakes perched precariously on the crowded mantel of the fireplace.

"It looks cozy." She smiled at him as she carefully picked her way across the toy-strewn floor to the spot on the couch.

"Yeah, that's one way to describe it." He said cheerfully. "Here, let me take your jacket."

She hesitated. "Oh um, okay. Thank you."

Logan watched as she shrugged out of the jacket. He frowned a little. The woman's hair and make-up were impeccable, and if her jacket and designer pants didn't cost as much as his couch he'd have been surprised. However, she was wearing a shirt that was obviously miles too big for her. She practically floated in it and as she handed him her jacket and sat down, nervously pulling the shirt away from her body, he cleared his throat.

"Can I get you something to drink? A cup of coffee or glass of water?" He draped her jacket across the pile of laundry on the chair.

"No, thank you."

She perched nervously on the edge of the couch, picking at the edge of her too-big blouse as Logan looked around for a chair. The rest of the furniture was covered in various items and he shrugged before grabbing one of the small chairs from Hazel's table.

Lily suppressed a smile as he sat his large body carefully in the chair. She wondered if the chair would hold his weight. He wasn't fat by any means, but he was the largest man she'd ever seen and she bit her lip as the chair creaked alarmingly under him.

"So, let's get started, okay?"

"Sure." She agreed.

He glanced at her empty hands. "Do you have a resume or references?"

She paled. "I um, no I don't. I didn't think to bring one. I haven't had a job in a while."

He nodded. "Alright. Well, why don't you tell me a bit about yourself?"

"Okay. My name is Lily Castro. I'm 25 years old and I'm a widow, as you know." She gave him a faint smile. He glanced at her bare left hand and she wondered if he found it strange that she wasn't wearing her wedding ring.

"I grew up in Jasper and uh, moved here to Wellings when I was fifteen. My dad had gotten a job at the mill here."

"That's a big change." He commented. "A big city to a small town must have been quite the adjustment."

"It was." She agreed. "My parents died when I was eighteen."

"I'm sorry." He murmured.

"Thank you. I uh, I married my husband shortly after that and I've spent the last few years being a homemaker."

She flushed brightly. It sounded incredibly lame, even to her. "I babysat a lot for neighbourhood families when I was a teenager, so I do have quite a bit of experience with babies and toddlers." She said a bit desperately. "I could um, I could probably get the names of some of the families and their numbers if you'd like to talk to them."

He nodded. "Sure. That would be great. So, why do you want to be a nanny?"

"I love children." She said eagerly as she glanced at Hazel. "And I, well I need to find a job rather quickly as well as a place to live, so I figured this position would be a good fit for me."

She paused and coloured again. "I – I'm assuming this is a live-in position?"

"Yes. I work three days on and four days off at the station. The three days I'm working, I'm living at the station so you'd be responsible for Hazel the entire time. During my four days off, I'll take care of Hazel and you'll be free to come and go as you please. If you want to stay somewhere else during those four days, you're more than welcome to."

"Oh, um...is staying somewhere else a requirement?" She said quickly.

He shook his head. "No. You're welcome to stay at the house. I just wanted to make it clear that you didn't have to, and that you wouldn't be responsible for Hazel when I'm at home."

"So, really it's just three days a week, then?" She asked.

"Technically, yes. Sometimes I do get called in to the station on my days off. If that happens and you're around, I'll ask you to look after Hazel."

"That wouldn't be a problem." She replied eagerly. "I won't mind at all."

"The pay is twelve hundred a month. You won't have to pay rent obviously, and all food costs are included as well."

She blinked a little. Twelve hundred seemed generous for a three day work week and her surprise must have shown on her face because Logan nodded.

"I know it seems like a lot for a part time position but please remember that you're responsible for Hazel for the entire three days. Not that I can't be reached or come home in an emergency, I can, but it does end up being a fairly large chunk of your time. As well, I'm asking you to do some light housekeeping and grocery shopping, and provide Hazel with nutritious meals and snacks. Can you cook?"

She nodded. "Yes and I'm fine with housekeeping and grocery shopping."

"Good. I'm looking for someone to start right away. What's your availability?"

"I can start immediately." She said quickly. "Whenever you need me to start."

"Alright." He hesitated and then glanced at Hazel. The little girl was completely ignoring them and he smiled fondly at her before turning back to Lily.

"Let's talk about Hazel. I'm sure you've noticed that she doesn't talk very much."

She nodded and watched curiously as his face darkened. "Actually, Hazel doesn't speak at all. Her mother died six months ago, Hazel was there when it happened, and she hasn't spoken a word since that day."

"Oh my gosh." Lily put her hand to her mouth and glanced again at Hazel. "That's terrible. I'm so sorry for the loss of your wife."

He nodded and leaned forward, letting his large hands dangle between his knees. "Other than the not talking, Hazel is a normal child. She has therapy twice a week and if they fall on the days that I'm working, I'll expect you to take her to them. I realize it'll be a bit tougher to communicate with her, but it's not impossible. She's pretty easy going."

"Okay." Lily answered.

He hesitated. "She does, occasionally, have nightmares. I um, I usually let her crawl into the bed with me when that happens so if I'm not there...."

"She can sleep with me if she's frightened in the night. That won't be a problem." Lily hastily assured him.

His cell phone rang and he grimaced before pulling it from his pocket. He glanced at it and gave her an apologetic look. "I'm sorry. I should take this."

"No problem." Lily smiled brightly at him as he stood and left the living room. She waited a moment before crossing to the small table and kneeling on the floor opposite of Hazel.

"That's a pretty picture, honey. You're really good at colouring." She said softly.

The little girl glanced at her and then dropped her gaze back to the picture in front of her.

"Would you mind if I coloured with you?"

The little girl didn't respond and Lily carefully selected a colouring book from the stack on the floor and picked out a crayon from the large tin can sitting on the table. Humming softly to herself, she began to colour. After a moment she glanced up. Hazel was staring at her and Lily smiled encouragingly.

"Could you pass me the green crayon please, Hazel?"

After about thirty seconds the little girl plucked a green crayon from the tin and handed it to her.

"Thank you." Lily said as she began to colour the field. The next time she looked up, Hazel had left her chair and drifted closer. She held a blue crayon in her hand and she was studying the picture in front of Lily.

"Maybe you could help me colour the sky?" Lily said quietly. "This is a pretty big picture and I could use some help."

Hazel didn't nod or look at her but after a few seconds, she began to colour the sky. Lily smiled happily. "That looks great. Thank you, Hazel."

She selected a purple crayon and quickly filled in the small flowers. "What do you think of the purple? I like purple. Maybe I should put some pink in there as well?" She asked without looking up.

A small hand, sticky with syrup, crept into her vision. It was holding a pink crayon and Lily took it with another nod. "Thank you, honey."

Logan stood in the doorway of the living room, his cell phone held loosely in one hand and his mouth slightly ajar. He'd had three different nannies since Erin died and Hazel hadn't gone near any of them. Hell, she had even closed herself off from Betty, the housekeeper she had known her entire life. He couldn't believe that Hazel was actually colouring with the woman.

He grinned happily to himself. He had found a nanny who Hazel seemed to like and it was –

He stopped mid-thought and stared at the woman's midsection. She was kneeling at the small table and her too-large shirt had been caught under her knees. It hugged her belly, showcasing the obvious bump and the feeling of relief that was surging through him, flew out the window.

"You're pregnant." He blurted out.

The woman looked up, clearly startled, before looking down at her stomach. She flushed and yanked her shirt free before standing up.

"I um – well, yes I am."

"How far along are you?" He asked bluntly.

"Six months." She whispered. "I – it won't affect my ability to do the job, Mr. Anderson. I promise you."

"Right." He sighed. He glanced at his watch again. "Well, thank you for stopping by, Lily. I should probably get started on some lunch for Hazel."

"Of course." She quickly put on her jacket before staring up at him. "Um, could I get your email address to send you the names of my references?"

"Uh, why don't you just give me your cell number and I'll text you my email address. I do have a few other people to interview for the position so, you know...." He trailed off.

Her face dropped and for one horrifying moment he thought she was going to start crying. She swallowed hard and blinked rapidly. "Right, of course."

She recited her number and he quickly added it to his cell before smiling at her. "Thank you again, Lily."

"Thank you." She said quietly. She took a deep breath and walked over to Hazel. She squatted carefully and held her hand out to the little girl. "Bye, Hazel. It was nice to meet you."

Logan's mouth dropped open when Hazel held her hand out and allowed Lily to shake it firmly. Lily touched her soft hair gently before standing and limping out of the living room. Logan followed her and stood there awkwardly as she tugged her boots on and put her hat and mittens on.

Without looking at him, she said softly, "Thank you again, Mr. Anderson. I – I hope to hear from you soon."

"Bye, Lily."

She slipped out the front door and he shut it firmly behind her before leaning against it for a few seconds. "Back to the drawing board, Logan." He muttered to himself before heading to the living room.

"Hazel? What do you want for – "

He stopped, his mouth dropping open again. Hazel was standing at the living room window and he followed her gaze. Lily, her head bent against the cold wind and blowing snow, was limping slowly down the sidewalk and Hazel was staring intently at her. She looked briefly at Logan before looking out the window again at Lily."

He hesitated a moment longer and then said, "Hazel – stay here. Daddy will be right back."

He jammed his bare feet into his boots and ran outside. "Lily! Lily! Wait up a minute."

She turned, and he jogged over to her as she quickly wiped at her face with the palms of her hands. "I'm sorry? Did I – did I forget something?"

He shook his head, staring at the tear tracks on her face. "No."

A gust of wind blew and he shivered in his thin t-shirt and jeans. "Where did you park?"

She stared blankly at him for a moment. "I – I don't have a car. I took the bus here."

He stared at the snow that was collecting on her pink hat and at her bright red cheeks before sighing. "Just let me get Hazel into her coat and boots and I'll give you a ride home."

"Oh no! That's fine. I don't need a ride." She protested.

"I don't mind. Come back to the house for a minute."

Without waiting for her answer, he turned and started back to the house. After a moment, Lily followed silently.

* * *

"There you go, baby bug. All strapped in." Logan kissed the tip of Hazel's nose and rechecked the straps to the car seat before sliding out of the back seat of the truck.

"Ready, Lily?"

She was standing at the passenger side of his truck and staring at the seat. The truck didn't have a running board, and she stepped closer before standing on her tiptoes and stretching for the handle at the top of the door. She could only just reach it, and she realized with shameful embarrassment that she wouldn't be able to lift herself into the truck. She was too short, her leg was too weak, and her stomach was too big.

"I'm sorry, I um, I don't think I can − could you maybe help me? My leg is still - I just need a bit of a boost." He had already slid behind the wheel and she gave him a look of painful embarrassment.

"Oh, of course. Sorry."

She held her hand out but instead of taking it like she expected, he slid back out and crossed quickly in front of the truck. He was standing behind her and cupping her elbows before she knew what was happening.

"Watch your head." He lifted her easily into the truck and she gave a small squeak of surprise as she landed with a thump on the seat.

"Okay?"

"Yes, thank you." She flushed again and stared out the window as he started the truck and backed out of the driveway.

* * *

"This is where you live?" Logan put the truck into park and stared at the mansion he was parked in front of. It was about three times the size of his house and had a large, three car garage attached to it. The driveway had been plowed of the snow, and the steps and pathway to the porch were shoveled clear as well.

Lily nodded as she unclicked her seatbelt. "Yes, sort of."

"Sort of?" He frowned.

"It belongs to my husband's family." She said briefly.

She reached for the door handle of the truck. "Thank you for the ride, Mr. Anderson."

"You're welcome."

She hesitated and seemed to gather her courage before turning back to him. "Mr. Anderson, I promise if you give me a chance, you won't regret it. I'm really great with children and I keep a neat house and I'm a pretty good cook. I've had a very normal, easy pregnancy and there really isn't anything I can't do because of it."

He sighed. "Lily, the thing is, I'll likely have you as a nanny for what – three months, tops? Once you have your baby, I'm sure you won't be interested in nannying for Hazel any longer. I'm looking for someone who can stick around until Hazel is in school. That's a year. Plus, if I did give you the job and Hazel became attached to you, it would be very difficult on her to have you leave in three months. She's already going through a rough time. I don't want to make it worse."

"Mr. Anderson – "

"Please don't take this the wrong way, but I'm not really sure why you need this job anyway. Your house is obviously expensive and, sorry I know this sounds rude, but you seem to be doing just fine in the money department. Why spend the last three months of your pregnancy looking after someone else's kid?"

She took a deep breath. "When my husband died he left everything to his parents. The house, the money, none of it is mine. I'm – well, I'm flat broke and I need a job and someplace else to live. Barry's parents have allowed me to stay in the house for a while now but they would prefer if I – if I found alternate living arrangements."

He gaped at her. "Are you kidding me? They want their son's wife and unborn child to move out of their home? What's wrong with these people?"

She sighed and rubbed at her forehead. "It's a very long story and really, not that interesting. The point is – I need a job and a place to live and I promise you I'll work very hard and take excellent care of Hazel."

When he didn't reply, she gave him a pleading look. Tears were starting to form in her eyes and she blinked them back. "Please, Mr. Anderson. I'm sorry. I hate to beg and I know how pathetic I look but I really need this job. I promise you I won't leave after the baby is born. I swear. I really won't. I won't even need to take any time off. I can just have the baby and go right back to work."

Despite her efforts to hold them back the tears were flowing down her cheeks now. "And I know that a baby can be noisy at night and I'll," she thought desperately for a moment, "I'll find another place to stay with the baby when you're not working." She finished anxiously.

"Where would you go?" He raised his eyebrow at her.

She swiped at the tears on her cheeks. "I could, I don't know, rent a motel room for the four days a week. You – you wouldn't even know the baby was there."

She gave him a desperate look edged with bright panic and he sighed before staring out the windshield of the truck. "Can I think about it?"

She nodded. "Of course. Thank you for thinking about it. I really appreciate it."

She smiled at Hazel before sliding out of the truck. He watched as she trudged carefully toward the front porch before he met Hazel's gaze in the rear view mirror.

"What do you think, Hazel? Do you want her to be your new nanny?" He asked, not expecting a reply.

He turned and stared at the little girl when she nodded solemnly. "Hazel, do you like Lily? Do you want me to hire her?"

The little girl nodded again and Logan threw open the door of the truck and slid to the ground. "Lily!"

She turned and gave him a trembling smile. "Yes?"

"I've thought about it. Can you start Monday?"

Her mouth dropped open and she stared wide-eyed at him for a moment before nodding. "Yes, I can absolutely start Monday."

Chapter 4

Logan threw open the front door and hurried down the steps. "Here, Lily. Let me help you with that."

Lily, pulling a large suitcase behind her and carrying her purse and an overnight bag, looked up. "Oh, it's fine." She puffed. "I've got it."

He ignored her and reached for the suitcase. "Did you take the bus here?"

"Yes." She adjusted the overnight bag on her shoulder and followed him up the steps.

"I could have picked you up. I thought you would take a cab here." He set the suitcase down in the hallway as Lily took her boots off before shrugging out of her jacket and hanging it neatly in the front closet.

"I don't mind." She said cheerfully. "The exercise is good for my leg."

He stared at the suitcase and the overnight bag. "Well, why don't I give you a lift back to get the rest of your things?"

"I – I don't have anything else."

He frowned at her. "This is all of it?"

"Yes. I'm sorry." She said quickly as she eyed him carefully.

"Sorry for what?" He gave her a confused look.

"Uh, I don't know." She said awkwardly.

"This is really all of your stuff?" He frowned again at her.

"Y-yes. I – most of the items in our home belonged to my husband and he left them to his parents." She gave him another oddly nervous look.

"Okay. Well uh, follow me. I'll show you to your room and give you a tour of the rest of the house." He started down the hallway as Hazel, carrying the same doll from the weekend, popped her head out of the living room.

"Hi, Hazel." Lily gave her a bright smile. "Do you think you could carry my purse for me?"

Hazel nodded and took the purse, slinging it over her arm before following Lily and her father up the stairs.

Logan paused at the head of the stairs and pointed to the door in front of them. "This is the guest bathroom. I have a bathroom off of my bedroom so this one is all yours."

He pointed to the door to the left. "That's a spare room. It's sort of my den/office/work out room."

She followed him down the hallway. "This is my room."

She peered in briefly at the large king-size bed and walnut-coloured wardrobe. The room was done up in very masculine colours which, considering he would have shared it with his wife, seemed a little odd to her but she didn't say anything as he continued down the hallway.

"This room is Hazel's." The room was painted a light purple and there was a small bed covered in princess sheets and a matching princess quilt against the far wall. The room was bright and cheery with colourful posters on the walls and various toys scattered across the floor.

"It's so pretty, Hazel." She smiled at the little girl and squeezed her thin shoulder. Hazel ducked her head and stared at the floor as Logan opened the last door.

"And this is your room."

Lily walked into the room and stared around in delight. It was a good size room with a double bed covered in a light gray quilt. A plain white dresser was against the wall and there was a tiny desk and chair pushed up under the large window. The walls were painted a creamy white.

"It's a bit bare." He said apologetically, but you can paint it and add your own personal touches to it. Whatever you'd like."

"It's perfect." She sighed happily. "I really like it."

He gave her a strange look that she didn't notice. "Well, it's not much but like I said, you can make it your own. Hazel knows that when I'm at home and you're in your room that she's not to disturb you."

"Oh, I won't mind." She said quickly.

He shook his head. "It's best if you have some of your own personal time as well, Lily. Hazel knows the rules and she'll follow them."

He tugged Lily's purse from Hazel and set it on the small desk before taking Hazel's hand. "We'll let you get settled in and unpacked. Dinner will be in about an hour or so if you'd like to join us."

"Do you need some help? I can – "

He shook his head again. "Nope. I'm keeping it simple tonight and I can handle grilled cheese and tomato soup." He hesitated. "Do you like grilled cheese sandwiches and tomato soup?"

"I do. Thank you." She gave him a sweet smile and he cleared his throat as an odd warmth filled his belly.

"Okay then, we'll see you in an hour." He and Hazel left the room, shutting the door quietly behind them.

Lily sat down on the bed and then flopped backwards. She stared up at the ceiling, a small smile crossing her lips. The room was beautiful and for the first time she was on her own and supporting herself. She couldn't be happier.

The baby kicked and she rubbed her expanding belly gently. "Hello, baby girl. Mama is going to give you a good life, I promise."

Her smile faltered. She had sent a brief email to Barry's parents, letting them know she was moving out but not giving them any other explanation. Her cell phone had sang its shrill cry as she was riding on the bus, and she hadn't needed to glance at the screen to know it was them.

She sighed. She would have to change her number. They would hound her relentlessly if she didn't. She rubbed her belly again. She would tell them when she had the baby. She was their grandchild after all and they deserved the right to know that she was born healthy and safe. She might even let them meet her.

She took a deep breath and closed her eyes. The important thing was that she didn't screw this up. She needed this job, it meant the difference between giving up and keeping her baby, and she would do whatever it took to keep her baby.

"No one's taking you away from me, sweet pea." She whispered as she stroked and caressed her belly. "No one."

* * *

"Come on, Hazel. Eat up, honey." Logan coaxed.

Lily glanced at the little girl before staring down at her own bowl of soup. She stirred it carefully, studying the lumps in it before spooning a sip of it into her mouth. She swallowed it with difficulty, it was so salty it made her mouth water, and hurriedly took a drink of water.

Logan stood and opened the kitchen window a bit wider. Lily had gone to the kitchen when she heard the shrill sound of the smoke alarm. She had stared in surprise at the scene in the kitchen. Logan was flapping a dish towel at the smoke alarm as he moved the pan from the stove. A blackened sandwich was smoking in the middle of it and he had tossed it into the trash before turning and smiling at Hazel.

"Don't worry, ma'am. I'm a firefighter."

Lily had snorted laughter and he had grinned at her before indicating she should sit down. "Just a small accident with the grilled cheese. Have a seat, the other ones have turned out."

Now, Lily stared at the grilled cheese sandwich on her plate. Although not as black as the one he had thrown in the trash, it was charred and crispy and she didn't think there was enough ketchup in the world to make it edible.

She took another sip of soup to be polite and couldn't hide the grimace from her face when she swallowed it. Luckily, Logan was still standing at the sink and didn't notice. Hazel, on the other hand, was staring at her and Lily winked at her before stirring the bowl of soup again.

"Hazel." Logan chided gently as he sat back down. "Eat your soup, please."

She shook her head and reached for the plate of cut-up carrots and celery. She munched on a carrot stick, staring from beneath her lashes at Lily.

Logan took a large spoonful of soup and Lily watched with amusement as he spit it back into the bowl, wiping his mouth and choking a bit. "Christ, that's terrible!"

He glanced at Hazel. "Sorry, baby bug. Daddy shouldn't curse."

He sighed and reached for his cell phone. "I'll order us some pizza."

Lily stood up. "I can make some grilled cheese if you have more bread?"

"I do, but you don't need to do that. I can order – "

"I don't mind. I like to cook." Lily smiled at him and walked to the fridge. She opened it and bent over, rummaging through the shelves. Logan eyed her ass. She was slender and her ass was small, but it looked firm and tight in her yoga pants.

He looked away quickly. Lily wasn't here for eye candy. She was here to look after Hazel and he would be smart to remember that.

She straightened, her arms full of various produce, and carried them to the counter. "I can make us a salad to go with the sandwiches."

She went to work quickly and within fifteen minutes, the smell of perfectly toasted grilled cheese filled the air. She cut a sandwich into four wedges and set it on Hazel's plate. "Here you go, honey. Try it."

Hazel stared at the sandwich. The bread was a perfect light brown and cheese was oozing out of the sides. After a moment, Hazel picked it up and bit gingerly into it. She chewed thoughtfully before swallowing and taking another larger bite.

Lily smiled with delight and set down a bowl of salad beside the sandwich. "Have some salad as well, Hazel."

She set the second sandwich in front of Logan. He took a big bite and gave her the thumbs up. "It's delicious."

She blushed brightly. "Thank you."

She cooked another two sandwiches and gave one to Logan before placing the last one on her plate. She ate quickly, dipping the sandwich into a small pool of ketchup. When she realized Logan and Hazel were watching her, she blushed again.

"What?"

"I've never seen someone dip their grilled cheese in ketchup before." Logan grinned at her.

Her blush deepened. "It's pretty good."

Logan took a bite of his sandwich and stared at Lily as he chewed. He had never met a woman who blushed as much as she did, and he was fascinated by the way her pale skin reddened into a perfect rose hue. Hazel was watching her as well and she suddenly pointed at the ketchup bottle.

"Do you want some ketchup too, Hazel?" Logan asked. She nodded and he squeezed some on to her plate. She dipped a corner of the sandwich into the ketchup before biting off the end of it.

"Do you like it?" Lily asked softly.

Hazel didn't acknowledge her but she dipped her sandwich into the ketchup again and took another bite.

Logan shrugged and squeezed some ketchup on to his plate. "When in Rome..."

* * *

She was awakened by the sound of Hazel screaming. She was on her feet, her heart pounding madly in her chest, and running to the door of her bedroom when she heard the heavy thud of Logan's footsteps running down the hallway. She opened the door and stood uncertainly in the hallway as Logan's deep voice came from Hazel's room.

"You're okay, baby bug. Shh, you're okay. Daddy's here. Don't cry." He appeared in the hallway, holding a crying, shaking Hazel in his arms, and jerked a little when he saw Lily standing in the hallway.

"Is she okay?" Lily whispered.

He nodded. "Yeah, she'll be alright. Sorry to wake you."

He carried Hazel into his bedroom and shut the door behind him. Lily went back to her room and crawled back into bed. Faintly, she could hear Hazel crying and the sound of Logan soothing her. After about five minutes, there was silence and she closed her eyes and tried to drift back to sleep.

* * *

"Okay, so — you've got my cell number and Betty's number if you need anything or if anything goes wrong. I mean, nothing will go wrong but if you need help just give me a call. Alright?" Logan said anxiously.

Lily smiled at him. "You bet. We'll be fine. Don't worry, Mr. Anderson."

"Call me Logan." He paused as he was pulling on his jacket. "Oh uh, I never asked – can you drive? Do you have your license?"

She nodded. "Yes, I have my license and I can drive."

"Great. My wife's car is in the garage. Please use it to run any errands or to take Hazel on outings. I'll call and have you added to the insurance, and the keys are hanging on the hook by the phone."

"Oh, um, thank you. That's very generous of you." Lily said, surprised.

"Don't mention it. Hazel's extra car seat is already set up in the back seat. She likes the library."

"Alright. I'll maybe take her there later this afternoon. Would you like that, Hazel?" She looked down at the little girl who was standing next to her.

Hazel shrugged without looking at her and Lily frowned a little. The little girl was pale and tired looking, and she seemed even more withdrawn this morning than ever.

Logan knelt down and kissed Hazel's cheek. "Daddy is going to work, honey. You're going to stay with Lily while I'm at work. You'll have lots of fun with her and when Daddy gets back we'll go to a movie together, alright?"

Hazel gave him a solemn look and Logan chewed at his lip worriedly before running his hand over her soft, blonde hair. "It'll be okay, baby bug. We'll face time later tonight so I can say goodnight to you."

He kissed her again and gave Lily a worried look as he stood up. "If Hazel has a nightmare – "

"She can sleep with me. I don't have a problem with that." She said immediately.

"Actually, what seems to have worked best in the past is if you bring her to my bed. You just have to sit with her until she falls asleep again." He said.

"Sure, I can do that." She smiled confidently at him. "It'll be fine. I'll call you if I need anything."

"Right. Okay, I'll talk to you later." Logan gave her a final worried glance before leaving the house.

Lily smiled down at Hazel. "Honey, do you want to help me make breakfast? I was thinking French toast. Have you made French toast before?"

Hazel shook her head but took Lily's hand when she held it out and followed her into the kitchen.

* * *

"Hazel! Look at you, baby girl! I swear you're getting bigger every time I see you!"

Logan whipped around at the sound of Rob's voice and stared in surprise at Lily and Hazel. They were standing in the doorway of the kitchen of the fire station, and Lily held Hazel's hand firmly in one hand and a plastic-wrapped loaf in the other.

She gave him a nervous look as Rob bent down and tickled Hazel lightly. "Hi, baby girl. Have you missed your Uncle Rob?"

Hazel ducked her head before burying her face into Lily's leg. Rob stroked her head affectionately and stood up. "Here, Lily. Let me take your jacket."

"Thank you." She took it off and handed it to him, blushing at the look of surprise on his face when he saw her belly.

Logan had crossed the room and he bent and scooped Hazel up. She smiled shyly at him before slinging her arm around his neck and resting her head on his broad shoulder. He rubbed her back as he gave Lily an anxious look.

"Is something wrong?"

"What? Oh – no, nothing's wrong. I just thought it would be nice for Hazel to visit with you quickly. I know you're home tomorrow but before we left for the library I asked her if she wanted to stop in and see you. She seemed excited by that." Lily said quickly.

"What's that?" Rob pointed to the loaf in her hand and she smiled nervously at him.

"I made some banana loaf and I thought maybe you guys would like some."

"Hell, yes!" Andy appeared beside her and he blinked at her belly before plucking the loaf of bread out of her hand. "Thanks, Lily!"

He carried it to the counter and elbowed an older man with a crew-cut. "Bill, slice this up."

"Are your hands broken?" Bill said mildly but began to slice the bread as Andy went to the fridge for the butter.

"I'm sorry." Lily whispered. "Should I have not brought Hazel here?"

Logan smiled reassuringly at her. "No, no. I'm glad you did. It's a nice surprise."

He patted Hazel's back gently. "So, everything's gone well?" He had spoken to Lily several times every day and face timed with Hazel every night, and Lily had assured him that everything was fine but he still needed to ask.

"Yes. Everything's been great. Hazel and I went to the mall and walked around yesterday, and today we went to the library. She picked out some new books. I told her you would read them to her tomorrow night before bed." Lily replied.

"I absolutely will." Logan grinned at Hazel and she kissed him softly on the cheek before resting her small head against his.

"Oh my God, this banana bread is delicious." Andy appeared beside them and shoved another piece of the bread into his mouth. "Does everything you bake turn out this good, Lily?"

She blushed brightly and Andy grinned at her. Logan's stomach tightened and he elbowed Andy lightly. "Enough, Andy."

Andy shrugged. "Just complimenting the lady, man."

"Yeah, yeah. Isn't there a truck you should be washing?" Logan said irritably.

Andy grinned at him before winking at Lily and walking away. Logan watched him walk away before turning back to Lily. She was giving him an anxious look and he made himself smile at her. "Thanks for the bread and for bringing Hazel by."

"You're welcome." She said softly. She held her arms out to Hazel. "Are you ready to go back home, honey?"

Hazel kissed Logan's cheek and then allowed Lily to take her. She wrapped her legs around Lily, just above her belly and put her arm around her shoulders. Relief rush through Logan. It was obvious that Hazel liked Lily, and some of the tension and stress he had been carrying lifted a little.

"Bye Logan. We'll see you tomorrow." Lily said as she set Hazel gently on her feet and picked up her jacket.

"You bet. Bye Hazel. I love you, honey. Be good for Lily." Logan watched them leave and jerked when Rob clapped him on the back.

"What are you doing, man?"

"What do you mean?"

"You hired a pregnant woman as your nanny?"

He shrugged. "She needed a job."

"Oh yeah?"

"Yeah."

Rob shook his head before glancing at Bill. "There he goes again."

"What's that supposed to mean?" Logan said indignantly.

"It means that you're being a white knight again."

Shut up, Rob." Logan said testily.

Rob shrugged. "You can deny it all you want but you've been like this since we've been kids. Always wanting to swoop in and save the damsel in distress."

"In case you've forgotten, I needed a nanny. Lily was the best candidate for the job."

"Really?" Bill had joined them and he gave Logan a shrewd look. "What happens when she has the baby? You gonna be one big happy family?"

Logan rolled his eyes. "She can still look after Hazel with a baby. I don't have a problem with babies, hell I love kids, so what do I care if there's another one in the house?"

"Are you telling me that Lily isn't in a desperate situation? That you didn't hire her because she fed you some sob story about how she was going to be out on the streets, pregnant and alone?" Rob asked skeptically.

Logan flushed and Rob looked to Bill. "Told you."

"Shut up, Rob." Logan sighed. "There's nothing wrong with helping a person out."

"No, there isn't. But you've been doing this your entire life and it's never really worked out for you. Has it, Logan? Do you want another Erin situation on your hands?" Rob asked quietly.

"Erin was different. Lily is nothing like her." Logan said tightly.

"I'm not saying she is. Listen man, I just don't want to see you get hurt again, that's all." Rob said gently.

"I'm not going to get hurt. Lily is Hazel's nanny, nothing more." Logan said firmly.

"Whatever you say, man. Whatever you say." Rob replied.

Chapter 5

Lily jumped out of her bed and limped quickly to Hazel's room. It was just after three in the morning and the little girl was screaming and thrashing in her bed.

"It's alright, honey. It's okay." She soothed as she picked up the screaming, twisting girl. She winced when one of Hazel's flailing hands caught her in the side of the head but held on grimly.

"Shh, baby. You're okay. Come on, I'll take you to your daddy's room. You can sleep in his bed." She lifted the little girl up and carried her down the hall to Logan's room. She slipped into the room, rubbing Hazel's back gently as the little girl clung to her.

"It's okay, my sweet one. It was just a bad dream. You're alright. No one's going to hurt you." She whispered as she sat on the side of Logan's bed and rubbed and patted the little girl's back. After about ten minutes, Hazel had stopped shaking and Lily pushed her back gently until she could wipe away the tears on Hazel's pale face.

"Better, honey?"

Hazel nodded and Lily kissed her sweet face before easing her into the bed. "Here, lay down and – "

Hazel made a high-pitched keening noise and grabbed anxiously at Lily.

"It's alright, honey. Shh, I'm not going anywhere. I'll sit right here until you fall asleep." Lily soothed.

Hazel shook her head rapidly and pulled on Lily's night shirt. She squirmed over in the bed and gave Lily a desperate look.

"Do you want me to lie down with you for a bit, honey?" Lily asked.

Hazel nodded and Lily climbed into the bed beside her. She pulled the sheets and the quilts up as the little girl wrapped her small body around her. She kissed the top of Hazel's head and rubbed her back gently.

"I'll stay right here, honey. Go to sleep. It'll be morning soon." She whispered.

* * *

Logan shut the front door and kicked off his boots before hanging his jacket in the closet. It was just after six in the morning and the house was still and quiet. He walked down the hallway and took a quick look into the living room. His jaw dropped. The formerly messy and cluttered living room had been cleaned. Hazel's toys were stacked neatly in the toy box and the piles of laundry had disappeared. The carpet had been vacuumed and the mantel above the fireplace had been reorganized and dusted. He wandered into the kitchen. The appliances gleamed and the floor looked like it had been freshly washed.

"Jesus." He whispered. He was pretty sure the house had never been this clean before. He ducked his head into the half bath on the main floor and shook his head at how shiny and clean it was. Moving quietly, he headed up the stairs. He would check quickly on Hazel before having a hot shower. He stuck his head into Hazel's room, his stomach dropping when he saw her empty bed. He felt a brief moment of panic and he tamped it down as he turned and nearly ran to his room.

The door was slightly ajar and he let his breath out in a harsh rush when he saw both Hazel and Lily curled up in his bed. They were sleeping soundly and he stood silently next to the bed, staring down at them. Lily was sleeping on her side, the covers pulled to her shoulders and one hand tucked beneath her cheek. A strand of dark hair was across her face and he was struck with the ridiculous urge to smooth it back. He clenched his hands into fists as his gaze moved to Hazel. She was glued to Lily's back. Her face was buried between Lily's shoulder blades and he could see the outline of her arm under the covers around Lily's waist.

He stared at them for a few more minutes before stripping his shirt off and dropping it into the laundry hamper at the end of the bed. He would have a hot shower and if they weren't awake by then, he would –

Lily suddenly twitched and he watched as she rubbed at her eyes before yawning and stretching. She sat up and stretched again and his eyes dropped to her breasts. She was wearing a thin white shirt and he could see the outline of her nipples against the fabric. His cock stirred in his pants and he cleared his throat loudly.

Lily made a quiet breathless scream and stared wide-eyed at him. "What - what are you doing in my room?"

"Um, it's my room." Logan replied.

"What? I don't – "

She glanced around the room, and made a small moan of dismay as she slid out of the bed and stood up nervously. Her hair was a dark cloud around her face and he could see the curve of her bare belly where her shirt had ridden up. She was wearing light pink shorts and he stared at her slender, pale thighs. Her right one was perfect but there was a long, twisting scar on her left one. It started in the middle of her shin and ran to the middle of her thigh and it was a dark rose colour.

He made himself raise his gaze to hers. She was staring at his naked chest, her cheeks a fiery red and her full mouth a perfect round 'o'.

"Lily?"

"I'm not a sex maniac!" She blurted out.

"What?"

"I mean – Hazel had a nightmare and so I brought her to your room like you said to do, and she wanted me to lie down in the bed with her so I did. I must have fallen asleep. I'm so sorry. I didn't mean to fall asleep in your bed. Please don't fire me."

"Lily, it's alright." He said soothingly as he held his hands up. "It's fine. Just calm down. I'm not going to fire you."

"I swear I didn't mean to fall asleep." She whispered.

"It's honestly okay. I'm glad you were there for Hazel, really." He said quietly.

"I – why aren't you wearing a shirt?" She whispered again.

He glanced at his bare upper body. "I was just going to go and have a shower."

"Oh, right." She crossed her arms across her chest and licked her lips. "I'll um, I'll just go back to my room."

She glanced quickly at the sleeping Hazel before she hurried from the bedroom.

* * *

Lily sipped at her tea and watched as the people in the mall hurried past her. Breakfast this morning had been excruciatingly uncomfortable. Despite his assurance that he wouldn't fire her, she had been mortified that he had found her in his bed. She kept reliving the conversation in her head, how she had blurted out that she wasn't a sex maniac and the look on his face when she had said it.

She sighed and took another sip of her tea. It wasn't just what she had said. She couldn't forget the way he had caught her ogling his naked chest. It was a strong argument for her being a sex maniac. He had a beautiful chest; she could admit that to herself. Barry hadn't been much taller than her and while he wasn't fat, he certainly hadn't looked like he was made of granite. Logan was big, really big, and he had a perfect six pack and broad shoulders and a chest covered with hair that she could easily imagine running her fingers through.

She blushed and stared down at her feet. Logan was her employer and she needed this goddamn job. She needed to keep her libido under control. Truth be told, she was a little surprised by it. She had never really had a high sex drive, a fact that Barry had reminded her repeatedly of, and she knew that was the reason Barry had started having affairs. To suddenly be so strongly attracted to someone, to find herself wondering what it would be like to climb on top of Logan and –

She covered her face with her hand. What was going on with her? Pregnancy hormones, she thought frantically. It must be the pregnancy hormones. It was as good of an explanation as any. Plus, Logan really was a good looking man. It wasn't that surprising that she found him attractive.

What she needed to remember was that the man had just lost his wife six months ago. Just because she didn't miss her husband, didn't mean that Logan didn't mourn for his wife. Besides that, he didn't find her attractive. Her pregnancy had made her the size of a house and even if she wasn't, Barry had always said that she wasn't that good looking. She had been lucky to land someone like Barry. Lucky that he had seen past her plain dark hair and oddly-shaped face, and too-small breasts and -

"Lily?"

She jerked, spilling hot tea on her hand, and looked up. Logan and Hazel were standing in front of her, and smiled at them as she groaned inwardly. After breakfast, Logan had bundled Hazel up and taken her to a park to go sledding. Worried that she would be encroaching on their alone time and not wanting to wear out her welcome at their home, she had decided it would be better if she wasn't at home when they returned. She hadn't received her first paycheque yet and she only had about twenty dollars to her name, but it didn't cost anything to people watch at the mall. Unsure of the rules about using his dead wife's car when she wasn't technically working, she had left it parked in the garage and used her limited funds to take the bus to the mall.

"Oh, hi!"

"Hi." Logan sat down as Hazel climbed into Lily's lap and rested her back against Lily's round stomach.

"What – what are you doing here?"

He shrugged. "Hazel was bored at home but it was getting colder out so I decided to take her to the mall. She needs some new pants. She's starting to outgrow her old ones."

Hazel twisted on Lily's lap and rested her hand on Lily's stomach. She rubbed it gently as Lily smiled at her.

"Hazel, don't do that, honey." Logan said quietly.

"I don't mind." Lily replied. "I um – I told her there was a baby growing in my belly. I hope that's okay."

"That's fine." Logan glanced at the people walking by before giving Lily a curious look. "How did you get here? The car was still in the garage."

"I wasn't sure what the rules were about using the car when I wasn't working so I thought, just to be on the safe side, I would take the bus." She replied.

He frowned. "You can use the car whenever you need to, Lily. Whether you're working or not."

"Alright, thank you." She smiled gratefully at him.

"Okay, well I guess we'd better get going." Logan stood and held his hand out to Hazel. "Come on, honey. Let's find you some new pants."

Hazel frowned and slid off Lily's lap before grabbing her hand. She held it firmly and stared at her dad.

"Hazel, it's time to go."

She pulled on Lily's hand and gave her a pleading look. Logan crouched beside her. "Hazel, this is Lily's day off. Remember?"

A pout crossed Hazel's face and her brow darkened as she stared down at the floor.

"Hazel, no pouting." Logan said sternly. "Lily can't hang out with you all the time. She has to have time to do her own thing."

"I wouldn't mind going with you." Lily said softly, unable to resist Hazel's silent plea. "If, you know, you don't mind me butting in on your time with Hazel?"

Hazel gave her father a hopeful look and Logan smoothed her hair back from her face. "I don't mind at all."

* * *

Lily picked up the soft pink sleeper and stared delightedly at it. It was adorable and she stroked it lightly before checking the price tag. The smile dropped from her face and she quickly placed the garment back on the shelf.

An uncharacteristic wave of self-pity washed over her. Babies were expensive and they required a lot of stuff. If she couldn't afford even a damn sleeper, how was she going to afford to buy a crib, diapers, just the essentials, never mind any extras?

It'll be fine, Lily. The baby won't even need a crib right away. Hell, your mom told you repeatedly about how she kept you in a laundry basket beside the bed when you were first born. You have three months to save up your money to buy the stuff the baby needs.

She reached out and picked up the pink sleeper again. She would check out a few of the thrift stores in town. Babies grew so fast that it was ridiculous to buy them brand new clothes anyway. There would be nothing wrong with buying second-hand.

And when you have to pay for a motel room four days a week after the baby's born? What will you do then? That'll eat into your paycheque and you'll never be able to save up for your own place. You won't be able to live with Logan forever. You have a year at the most before Hazel starts school and he won't need you. Then it's finding a new job and daycare costs and rent. How are you going to do that?

She swallowed, feeling tears threatening again, and blinked rapidly. She was so tired of crying and it wasn't like it was going to help her solve any of her problems. She just had to take one day at a time, and not waste time and energy freaking out about what would happen a year from now.

"That's cute." Logan's voice spoke in her ear and she jumped guiltily before putting the sleeper back.

"Yeah, it is." She squeezed Hazel's hand when the little girl stepped beside her and took her hand. "Did you find some pants?"

"We did." Logan confirmed. "And they look dashing. Don't they, Hazel?"

The little girl smiled and rested her head on Lily's stomach.

"So do you know what you're having or are you just admiring the pink?" Logan asked.

"I'm having a girl. I found out at the last ultrasound appointment."

"Congratulations! That's wonderful!" Logan said enthusiastically.

"Thank you." Lily grinned at him. "I'm pretty happy about it."

Logan picked up Hazel and nuzzled her cheek. "This calls for a celebration. How about we grab some lunch?"

"Oh um, I'd better not. I don't have – I mean…"

Lily trailed off, her cheeks flushing as she gave him an uncomfortable look. She couldn't afford to go out for lunch but she didn't want to admit that to Logan.

"I insist. It's lunch time and you should eat. My treat." Logan said. "What do you think, Hazel? Should we go out for lunch today?"

Hazel nodded and Logan grinned at them both. "Great. Let's pay for Hazel's dashing new pants and go. Are you going to buy that sleeper?"

Lily shook her head. "No, not today."

"Alright. Well, let's go." Logan kissed Hazel's cheek and headed for the counter as Lily followed them.

Chapter 6

Lily opened the door to her bedroom and stared in surprise at Hazel. "Hazel? Honey, what's wrong?"

The little girl was sitting on the floor outside her door, holding her doll and two books, and she shrugged before standing. She took Lily's hand as Lily's nose crinkled.

"What is that smell?" Faintly, she could hear Logan's deep voice singing a country song as the sounds of pots banging came from the kitchen.

"Oh dear. Is your father trying to cook again?"

Hazel nodded and made a face. Lily laughed. "Do you want to hide in my room?"

She grinned eagerly and trotted into Lily's room, climbing up on to the bed and sitting cross-legged on it as Lily shut the door firmly behind her.

* * *

"Hazel! Dinner!" Logan stuck his head into the living room. It was empty and he jogged up the stairs and walked to Hazel's room.

"Baby bug? It's dinner time. Come and – "

He blinked in surprise. Hazel's room was empty and he quickly checked the bathroom and his room before staring down the hallway. Where was she? She wouldn't have gone outside and –

His gaze fell on Lily's door and he sighed before knocking on it.

"Come in."

He opened the door and sighed again. Lily was sitting cross-legged on the bed, her back supported against the wall by pillows and she was holding one of Hazel's books in her hands. Hazel leaned against her, one small hand lazily rubbing Lily's belly as she stared at the book.

"Baby bug, you know the rules." Logan said sternly.

Hazel's lower lip began to tremble as he moved closer to the bed. "When Lily is in her room, you don't disturb her."

"I invited her in." Lily said quickly. "She didn't break the rules."

Logan gave her a suspicious look and she smiled brightly at him. "It's true."

He dropped his gaze to Hazel who gave him a decidedly smug look before resting her cheek against Lily's belly.

"Lily, I hope you don't feel like you need to entertain her when it's your day off." Logan said.

"I don't." Lily replied. "I like being with Hazel. She's sweet and – "

She grinned when Hazel suddenly jumped and sat up. She looked at Lily's belly in surprise and Lily stroked her hair. "Did you feel that, honey? That was a big kick wasn't it?"

Hazel continued staring at her belly and Lily took her small hand. "Here, she's still moving around. Put your hand here."

She pressed Hazel's hand to her belly and Hazel's eyes widened before she grinned at Lily.

"Pretty neat, huh?" Lily grinned back. "This baby girl of mine is a mover and a shaker. I think I might be in trouble when she's born."

She glanced at Logan. He was staring at her belly with a strange look of longing on his face and she said hesitantly, "It must remind you of when your wife was pregnant with Hazel. Was Hazel active?"

He didn't reply and she touched his shoulder tentatively. "Logan?"

"I uh – I don't really know. Erin didn't like to have her belly touched when she was pregnant." He said gruffly.

Lily frowned. That seemed strange to her. Not that she wanted complete strangers touching her belly, which had happened twice already, but the father of her child was a different story. She had grown to loathe Barry near the end but she wouldn't have denied him the joy of feeling his unborn child moving in her belly.

Logan was still staring at her belly and she made a sudden decision. "Here, would you like to feel her kicking?" She took his hand and placed it on her belly before he could protest.

The baby chose that moment to deliver a particularly strong kick and she watched as a look of amazement crossed Logan's face. "That's so cool." He whispered.

Still pressing his hand against her belly, he sat down on the side of the bed beside her and stared at her belly. "I – that's just so cool." He repeated.

Hazel pressed her hand above her father's and Lily smiled at her. "I think she's moved to the other side, honey."

She slid Hazel's hand to the left, just below her ribcage, and didn't object when Logan eagerly placed his hand beside Hazel's. The baby kicked again and Hazel and Logan exchanged mutual looks of delight.

"Did you feel that, Hazel?" He said. "That's the baby." He leaned forward until his face was only inches from Lily's belly. "Hello baby. Are you a good girl? Are you a sweet little baby?" He rubbed her belly lightly as Hazel placed another soft kiss on her belly.

Lily stared at him in surprise, feeling a weird warmth infusing her body. She knew Logan was kind, she knew he loved children, but to see him cooing and talking to the baby growing inside her body was making her feel strange and happy all at the same time. Even if Barry had lived, he would never have acted this way about the baby, she was sure of it, and she felt a moment of bitterness. How different her life would have been if she had married someone like Logan. If she had –

She realized that Logan had put both of his big hands on her belly and was rubbing in gentle circles. Although it was odd, her employer rubbing and caressing her belly, she couldn't bring herself to ask him to stop. The look on his face was one of child-like wonderment and besides, she admitted to herself, she liked how it felt. For such a big man, he was surprisingly gentle, and his warm hands felt wonderful on her belly. She wished she wasn't wearing a t-shirt, wished she could feel his hands directly on her skin and hear the soft rasp as his callused palms glided across her skin.

She was so warm she was nearly sweating. In her mind's eye she could see Logan's hands stroking the naked skin of her belly. She bit down on her lower lip as she imagined them moving higher, imagined them cupping her naked breasts, his fingers running over her nipples until they were hard and aching and –

She had been reclining against the pillows as Logan and Hazel touched her belly and, with a small gasp, she sat up straight. Logan pulled his hands away and gave her a look of embarrassment. "I'm sorry, Lily. I shouldn't have – "

She shook her head. "No, it's fine really. I didn't mind."

The baby kicked again and Hazel, who was still resting her hand on Lily's belly, smiled broadly and kissed her belly once more.

Lily, feeling flushed and odd and desperate to get away from Logan, cleared her throat. "I should probably have something to eat so – "

"Right, of course." Logan stood up from the bed. "Would you like to join us for dinner? I've made plenty and – "

"Oh no, no. I didn't mean to — I wasn't angling for a dinner invitation." Lily blurted out. "I was just going to make myself a salad."

Logan shook his head. "I've already cooked. You might as well join us. I've made a chicken and cheese casserole. It's Hazel's favourite. Isn't that right, baby bug?"

Hazel gave Lily a look of such weary resignation that Lily had to manufacture a cough to hide her giggles. The look clearly indicated that she believed Lily should suffer along with her, and she couldn't resist Hazel's silent plea.

"Well, if you're sure you don't mind, I'd love to join you." She winked at Hazel and took her hand, allowing the little girl to lead her towards the kitchen.

* * *

Lily stared down at the gooey mess on her plate. Logan had said it was chicken and cheese casserole and she believed him but it looked strange to her. There were big chunks of cheese floating in it and she poked gingerly at the weird green blobs of what she thought might have been broccoli.

"Eat up, Hazel." Logan said encouragingly. The little girl was staring down at her plate, a fork in one hand and she glanced at Lily.

Lily put some of the goo on her fork and nodded to Hazel but couldn't actually bring herself to raise the fork to her mouth.

Logan glanced at her. "What?"

"Nothing. It uh, it looks really good." She lied.

"Right." He popped a forkful into his mouth and she watched as he turned bright red before standing up and spitting the mouthful into the garbage.

"Don't eat that." He advised. "I think I might have used too much salt."

He took Hazel's plate and scraped the food into the garbage as Lily grinned at him. "Why don't I make us something?"

"You don't have to do that. I can make sandwiches and – "

"I don't mind." Lily was already standing and heading to the pantry. "I can whip something up in half an hour. Hazel, would you like to help me cook dinner?"

Hazel nodded and dragged the small wooden stool underneath the table over to the counter. She stood on it as Lily pulled out some pasta from the pantry, a head of garlic and a jar of crushed tomatoes. "Do you guys like pasta?"

"Yes." Logan answered. He took a sip of beer and watched as Lily took out a package of ground beef from the freezer, popped it into the microwave and set it to defrost.

"Normally I make meatballs but that'll take too long. We'll just do a ground beef in sauce this time and next time I'll make meatballs." She told Hazel.

She pulled some mushrooms and yellow pepper from the fridge. She rummaged through the drawer and came up with a small, round brush. "Hazel, you can brush the mushrooms clean while I cut up the pepper and the garlic."

* * *

"Damn, that was good." Logan groaned as he sat back in his chair. "You're a really great cook, Lily."

"Thanks." She blushed. "Would you like some more?"

"No. I think two plates is my limit." He rubbed his flat stomach and winked at Hazel. "Daddy's going to get fat eating like this."

"I'm so sorry!" Lily said anxiously. "I do tend to use a lot of butter and oil when I cook. I know it's not the healthiest but I can find some new recipes that are healthier."

Logan gave her an odd look. "No, that's alright. We really like your cooking. Don't we, Hazel?"

Hazel nodded and gave Lily a thumbs up. Lily smiled at her. "Thank you, honey."

"I feel bad, though." Logan admitted. "You shouldn't have to cook for us on your day off."

Lily shrugged and began to clear the table. "I like to cook and it's a lot easier to cook for three people instead of just one. I'll be cooking anyway so I could be in charge of the meals."

He didn't reply and she gave him a careful look. "I mean, if that's alright with you."

He grinned at her. "It's more than alright with me. As long as you're sure you don't mind?"

"Not at all." Lily said firmly as Logan stood and helped her load the dishwasher.

"Great!" Logan smiled at her and she gave him a shy look.

"If you let me know what you like, I can make some meal plans and do some grocery shopping tomorrow."

"We like whatever. We're not picky." Logan said cheerfully. He paused and then reached into his back pocket. He pulled out a cheque, it was a bit wrinkled, and handed it to her. "Here."

"What's this?" She blinked in surprise at the cheque.

"It's your wages for the month."

"But – but I've only been working for three days." She stammered.

He shrugged. "I know. I'm fine with paying you early. I'm pretty sure you're not going to take the money and run."

"What? No, I would never do that to you!" She gasped.

He patted her arm lightly. "I'm just teasing you, Lily."

"Right." She blushed.

He gave her a quick look. "I was going to take Hazel to the new Disney movie tomorrow. Would you like to join us? I know Hazel would really like it if you did."

She nodded. "Thanks. I'd like that too."

"Great. It's a date." Logan said cheerfully.

* * *

"Logan, are you sure about this? I mean, it really sounds like more of a family thing." Lily protested as Logan lifted Hazel into the truck and buckled her securely into her car seat.

"I'm positive." Logan replied. "Janet specifically invited you as well."

He stood behind Lily and lifted her easily into the truck. "I've really got to get a running board." He muttered to himself as he crossed to the driver's side and climbed behind the wheel.

"Although," he eyed her growing belly, "I'm not sure that you could get into the truck even with a running board."

Lily gave him a mock scowl. "Watch it, mister. I might be fat and have a bum leg but I'm tougher than I look."

He laughed and rubbed his hand along the unfamiliar smooth skin of his jaw. "I'm shaking in my boots, ma'am."

"You look different without your beard." Lily said suddenly.

"Good different or bad different?" He had shaved the beard off for the first time in nearly a year. Erin had hated the beard, and he had to admit to himself that although he liked the beard, the real reason he had kept it was to tick her off. Of course, he refused to admit that yesterday morning as he had stared at the razor in his hand, he had been thinking of Lily and wondering if she hated beards too.

"Just different." She replied.

"You don't like it?"

She shrugged. "I liked the beard."

He didn't reply and she gave him a small smile before staring out the windshield. She was nervous about going to Rob and Janet's house. It had been a month since she had started working for Logan and while they had settled into a comfortable routine, she didn't know that it was appropriate for her to be tagging along to his friend's house for dinner.

"Logan, are you sure about this?" She asked softly.

He nodded. "Yes. I told you – Janet specifically invited you. Stop worrying, Lily. Janet is a very nice lady and I have a feeling you two will get along great."

* * *

"Lily! It's so nice to finally meet you." Janet was short and chubby with long red hair and pale, freckled skin. She shook Lily's hand firmly as a toddler clung to one leg and a child of about seven hid behind her.

"It's nice to meet you as well." Lily said shyly.

"Rob's been raving about your baking for weeks now. I hear you make a mean apple pie."

Lily blushed. "Oh, I don't know about that."

"It's true." Logan wandered over and kissed Janet's cheek affectionately. "It's not just the baking either. She's also a great cook."

He squeezed Lily's shoulder briefly and Lily's blush deepened. Neither noticed the considering look Janet gave them before she picked up the toddler and kissed her cheek. "This is Nicole and the kid hiding behind me is Derek."

"Hi there." Lily said. "My name is Lily."

Rob stuck his head into the kitchen. "Logan? The game's on and I've got a beer with your name on it." He paused. "What's with the smooth face?"

Logan shrugged before glancing at Lily. "Just thought I'd try something different."

"You look twelve years old." Rob snickered.

"Yeah, yeah. At least I can grow a beard." Logan rolled his eyes before leaving the kitchen.

Lily looked down as Hazel rested her head against her stomach.

"Hi, Hazel." Janet said kindly. "How are you, baby girl?"

Hazel hid her face against Lily's belly and Lily stroked her hair softly before smiling at Janet.

"She really likes you." Janet said quietly. "That's good. I'm glad to see it."

She turned to Derek. "Honey, why don't you take Nicole and Hazel down to the basement to play? I think your brother and sisters are down there."

"Alright, mama." Derek said agreeably.

He held his hand out to Hazel. "C'mon, Hazel."

Hazel glanced up at Lily and she gave her a reassuring smile. "Go on, Hazel. I'll be in the kitchen if you need me."

Hazel nodded and took Derek's hand. He led them out of the kitchen and Janet smiled brightly at Lily.

"Why don't you have a seat? Can I get you some tea? It's about half an hour until dinner."

"Sure, I'd love some." Lily sat down at the kitchen table as Janet flipped the kettle on.

"So, Logan says that you and Rob have five children?"

Janet nodded. "That's right."

"You must be very busy." Lily grinned at her.

"Yeah, that's one word for it. I love it though." Janet sat down at the table and eyed Lily's belly. "Can I ask how far along you are?"

"Just over seven months." Lily rubbed her belly gently.

"Congratulations." Janet replied. "So, will you keep working for Logan after the baby is born?"

Lily nodded. "Yes. I – I know it'll be a bit more difficult with a newborn but I'm confident I can handle it. Hazel's a very easy child."

"She is." Janet agreed. "I babysat her a few times after Erin died. She's doing much better now. She was almost completely unresponsive in the first few weeks. Has she spoken yet?"

Lily shook her head. "No. Her therapist gave me a few ideas and techniques to try out but none of them have worked so far. I'm trying not to push her into talking but it's hard. I want her to be able to communicate with us, you know?"

Janet nodded. "I do know." She poured them both cups of tea and returned to her seat. She dipped the tea bag in and out of the mug, swirling it in the hot liquid. "So, Rob says that you're a widow?"

"Yes."

"I'm sorry for your loss."

"Thank you." Lily looked down at her own tea as Janet cleared her throat.

"Do you like working for Logan?"

"Oh yes." Lily said eagerly. "He's a very nice man."

"He is." Janet agreed. "Not all women appreciate that."

"What do you mean?" Lily asked curiously.

Janet shrugged. "It's just that sometimes women can take advantage of Logan's good nature."

Lily's hands were turning to ice and she swallowed thickly. "I would never do that." She whispered.

Janet gave her a startled look. "Oh! Oh, honey. I didn't mean you, I swear. I can see that you're a lovely person and would never take advantage of him."

"Did – did Erin take advantage of him?" Lily asked hesitantly. In the last month she had often wanted to ask Logan about his dead wife but she couldn't think of a way to do it without coming across as nosy. She was nosy, though. There were no pictures of Erin anywhere in the house and Logan didn't act like a man who was mourning for his wife. Of course, she wasn't acting like a woman mourning for her husband so she certainly wasn't going to judge him for that.

"Has Logan told you anything about her?" Janet asked.

Lily shook her head. "No."

"Well, it's not my place to talk about their relationship but I will say that Erin wasn't very good for Logan or Hazel. I know this sounds like a terrible thing to say but both of them are better off without her." Janet said darkly.

Lily blinked at her. She was more curious now than ever about Logan's wife but Janet had already stood up and was opening the oven door. The delicious smell of roast beef filled the kitchen and Janet smiled at her. "I hope you're hungry. I've got enough food for a small army."

* * *

"Did you have fun tonight, Lily?" Logan asked as he drove carefully down the icy streets.

"I did." Lily answered. "Janet is really nice."

She stared out the window of the truck. Janet had asked her to go for coffee next week and she had been both nervous and pleased by it. She hadn't had a real friend since high school, and she was absurdly excited about having a woman friend again.

"How about you, Hazel? Did you have fun?" Logan asked.

There was a moment of silence and Lily jerked with surprise when a soft voice said, "Yes."

She stared wide-eyed at Logan. He returned the look, his face a mask of surprise and delight and, without thinking, she reached out and took his hand. He squeezed it tightly before smiling at Hazel in the rear view mirror.

"That's good, honey. I'm glad."

Lily's heart was hammering in her chest and she wanted to turn around and grin at Hazel but she made herself stare straight ahead. She continued to hold Logan's hand and he squeezed it again as Hazel cleared her throat.

"Lily?"

"Yes, honey?"

"When are you going to have your baby?"

"In a couple more months."

"Are you going to leave after that?"

She turned and gave Hazel a reassuring smile. "No, honey. I'm not. I'll still be your nanny even after the baby is born."

"Okay." Hazel stared out the window for a few minutes before she glanced at Logan.

"Daddy?"

"Yeah?" Logan's voice was hoarse and Lily could see tears gleaming in his eyes. She squeezed his hand again and gave him a trembling smile. She could feel tears in her own eyes and she blinked rapidly, trying to prevent them from slipping down her cheeks.

"Can I have some ice cream when I get home?"

"Yeah, baby. You can have some ice cream." He replied. "We all can."

Chapter 7

"Lily, let me take that for you. You shouldn't be carrying that." Logan hurried to take the large wicker laundry basket from Lily's hands. It had two plastic shopping bags in it and he carried it over to the couch.

Lily laughed. "It's not heavy, Logan."

She limped across the room and collapsed on the sofa. Logan placed the basket on the floor beside her. "You're limping more today."

Lily shrugged. "I think I strained it yesterday when I took Hazel sledding. It'll be fine. I just need to rest it."

Hazel leaned against her leg and stared with interest at the shopping bags. "What did you buy, Lily?"

"I bought some clothes for the baby." Lily said brightly. "Would you like to see them?"

Hazel nodded and Lily carefully emptied the bags on to the couch beside her.

Logan frowned. Lily was nearly eight months pregnant and this was the first time he had seen her buy anything for the baby. The bags were from the local thrift store and as Lily began to lay the clothing out for Hazel to look at, he frowned again.

"This is pretty!" Hazel stroked a tiny pink shirt and Lily grinned at her.

"I thought so too."

"It smells funny." Hazel sniffed at the shirt.

"It'll be fine once I wash it." Lily shrugged.

"What's this for?" Hazel had climbed into the laundry basket and was sitting in the bottom of it.

"It's a bed for the baby." Lily said absentmindedly as she sorted through the clothes.

"Babies sleep in cribs." Hazel replied.

"Not for the first little while." Lily said. "The baby will be small and she can sleep in the basket beside my bed."

"That's weird." Hazel announced. "Clothes go in laundry baskets, not babies."

"Hazel." Logan chided gently.

"What? They do." The little girl gave him a look of confusion. "Babies sleep in cribs." She repeated.

Lily was starting to look a little flustered. "That's right, they do. But sometimes they sleep in bassinets when they're first born. She won't need a crib until she's a bit older."

"This is a laundry basket." Hazel pointed out.

Lily laughed. "I know. Bassinets are expensive though and my mom said I slept in a laundry basket for the first two months, so I'll just use the laundry basket and then I'll have more money for a crib." She glanced quickly at Logan.

He was frowning at her and she felt a flush of embarrassment. "I'll have lots of added expenses with diapers and clothing and stuff. I thought it would be best to save money wherever I can."

He nodded but didn't say anything and she stared down at the second-hand baby clothes. She could feel the bite of tears and she blinked them back fiercely. There was nothing wrong with buying second-hand stuff for the baby. It didn't mean she didn't love her any less.

"Lily? Are you alright?" Logan asked quietly.

She nodded without looking at him. "Yes. My leg is just a little sore. I'm going to go throw these in the wash."

She gathered the clothes and limped out of the room as Hazel climbed into Logan's lap. "Daddy?"

"Yeah, baby bug?"

"Does Lily love me?"

He nodded. "Yes, she does."

"I love her too." The little girl leaned against him. "Do you think she'll love the new baby more than me?"

Logan hesitated. "I think Lily has enough love for both of you, honey."

"Really?"

"Yes."

"Do you think she'll let me hold her baby?"

"I'm sure she will." Logan replied.

"I'm going to go ask her." Hazel slid off his lap and skipped out of the room. Logan watched her go. It had been two weeks since Hazel had started speaking again and he still felt a little thrill go through him every time he heard her sweet voice. He stared moodily out the window. He had no doubt that Lily had played a large part in Hazel's recovery and he was more grateful to her than he could say. Still, he felt a small niggle of worry in his belly. He was pretty sure that Lily wouldn't leave after she had her baby but he worried about how Hazel would react if he was wrong. She had formed a strong attachment to Lily and he was afraid she would take it badly if Lily did leave.

She won't leave. She needs the money. She's going to give birth in a month and a half and she's bought hardly any baby supplies. She's shopping for baby clothes at thrift stores and planning on putting the baby in a laundry basket for God's sake.

He suddenly jumped up and climbed the stairs. He stared up thoughtfully at the attic door access, scratching lightly at the beard he had immediately regrown after Lily had mentioned she liked it, and then jumped a little when he felt Hazel's hand on his leg.

"Daddy? What are you doing?"

"Just thinking." He smiled down at her. "Did you ask Lily about holding the baby?"

"Yes. She said I could hold her and help give her baths and everything!" Hazel said excitedly.

"That's good, honey." Logan took her hand and led her back down the stairs. "Come on. It'll be dinner soon and I think we should help Lily cook tonight. Her leg is sore."

* * *

Hazel's terrified screams woke him from his own nightmare and he stumbled out of bed and staggered quickly down the hall. Hazel hadn't had a nightmare for weeks now and hearing her crying and screaming in the dark was heartbreaking.

He entered her room and nearly ran to the bed. "It's okay, honey. You're okay." He said as he plucked her from her bed.

"Daddy!" She clung to him, shaking wildly, and he kissed her damp cheek and rubbed her back as he carried her back to his room.

"It's alright, baby bug. Daddy's right here. Don't cry." He said soothingly.

"I want Lily!" Hazel sobbed.

He climbed into his bed and held Hazel's shaking body against his. "Shh, honey. It's okay."

"I want Lily, daddy!" Hazel continued to sob. "Please, I want Lily."

"She's sleeping, Hazel. It's really late. You can see her in the morning, okay?"

"No." The little girl cried harder. "Please daddy, I want Lily! Can we go to her room? Please, daddy. Please!"

"No, baby bug. I'm sorry." Logan winced when Hazel burst into loud, wailing sobs. "Honey, stop. You can't see Lily right now. You can – "

"I want Lily!" Hazel screamed hysterically and beat at his chest with her tiny fists. He tried to hold her flailing hands down and she screamed Lily's name again. He had never felt so helpless in his life, and he was just thinking about taking Hazel to Lily's room when Lily limped into his.

"It's okay, Hazel. It's alright, I'm here." She soothed.

"Lily!" Hazel sobbed loudly and held her arms out. "Lie down with me." She pleaded.

Lily hesitated and then climbed into the bed next to Hazel. The little girl practically leaped into her arms and Lily kissed her face repeatedly as she snuggled the little girl into her chest. "Shh, baby. You're okay. It was just a bad dream."

"Daddy..." Hazel whimpered. She reached behind her and tried to pull Logan closer.

He moved forward, pressing his chest against Hazel's back and kissing the back of her head. Hazel was sandwiched between them and he could feel Lily's warm breath on his face as he rubbed Hazel's side.

"You're okay, Hazel." He whispered.

The little girl made a watery, sobbing gasp in reply and clung tightly to Logan's hand as she buried her face in Lily's neck. Lily continued to rub her back, her hand brushing against Logan's naked chest with every stroke, and rested her cheek on the top of Hazel's head.

She made soothing, nonsensical sounds of comfort until Hazel's shaking had stopped. She stroked the little girl's hair.

"Better, honey?"

"Yeah." Hazel whispered.

"Good." Lily kissed her forehead. "I'm going to go back to my room now, baby. I'll see you in the – "

"No!" Hazel's voice was bright with panic and she clung grimly to Lily. "Don't leave me, Lily."

Lily glanced at Logan, her heart breaking a little at the look of helplessness on his face. She smiled reassuringly at him before kissing Hazel's cheek again. "Alright, honey. I'll stay here with you. Go to sleep."

"Promise you'll never leave me, Lily." Hazel whimpered.

Lily hesitated and glanced at Logan. He was staring at her, his eyes dark and unreadable, and after a moment, she whispered, "I promise I'll never leave you, Hazel."

* * *

Lily sighed happily and pressed her sore back against the heating pad. Her lower back ached all the time now, and the heat radiating into it felt delicious. She squirmed a little closer to it. Dimly, she wondered what type of heating pad was large enough to heat her entire back, but then decided she didn't care. The heat really did feel wonderful and she was just drifting back to sleep when something hard and warm cupped her breast.

She forced her heavy eyelids up. She stared in confusion at the wall before the night came rushing back to her. She had been woken by Hazel's screams and when Hazel had started screaming for her, she hadn't been able to ignore her desperate cries. She had climbed into bed with Hazel and Logan and —

She paused, her eyes widening as she slowly looked down. The last thing she remembered was falling asleep with Hazel's small body pressed up against hers and the sound of Logan's soft snoring in her ears. She realized with something close to horror that the heating pad against her back was Logan's body, and his large hand was cupping her breast firmly.

Hazel! Where was Hazel?

She scanned the room and was just in time to see the little girl, yawning hugely, disappearing out the door. She heard her walk down the stairs and after a moment, the faint sounds of the TV.

She swallowed and stared blankly at the wall. She was in her employer's bed and he was spooning her and cupping her breast. What the hell did she do now?

You get out of his bed before he wakes up and fires you for being a sex maniac, you idiot!

Right. Excellent idea.

She eased the covers back, desire pooling in her belly at the sight of Logan's hand cupping her breast through her thin t-shirt. Despite her fear that she would be fired, her desire was growing and she could feel her nipple hardening against his palm.

Shit. Get out of the bed, right now!

Before she could move, Logan snorted sleepily and pulled her closer. One large thigh crossed over hers, and she winced a little when he pressed against her left one. The pain was forgotten when he kissed her neck and squeezed her breast tightly.

She gasped when he plucked at her hardening nipple and her back arched helplessly when he tugged the loose neckline of her shirt downwards and her breasts popped free. Her nipples were hard and throbbing, and she couldn't tear her gaze away from them as she watched his thumb circle around one tight nipple.

Her lower body was on fire with need and excitement and when he made a low groan she turned her head and stared into his dark brown eyes. They were hazy with need and confusion and he blinked at her before whispering hoarsely, "Lily?"

She pressed her mouth against his, pushing her tongue at his lips, and he groaned and opened his mouth as his hand tightened around her breast. With a low growl he pushed her on to her back and shoved his thigh between hers. He stared down at her naked breasts for one hot moment before kissing her hard.

She wrapped her arms around his broad shoulders, clinging tightly to him as their tongues stroked and rubbed against each other's. He cupped her left breast, pulling hard on her nipple as she arched her back and whimpered into his mouth.

He sucked on her bottom lip until she moaned and then trailed a path of kisses down her neck.

"Logan." She moaned again.

"Lily." He whispered. He traced her collarbone with the tip of his tongue and she gasped and rubbed her pelvis against his hard thigh. His hand moved to her belly and he rubbed it through her shirt, caressing it gently as he kissed a path of wet, hot kisses over her chest. He stopped just above her breast, and she made another soft cry and arched her back, trying to press her nipple against his mouth.

He made a low noise of need before sucking her hard and swollen nipple into his mouth. He rubbed the tip of it against his tongue and she clutched at his short hair, her fingers digging into his scalp.

"Logan, that – that feels so good." She whispered.

"You're so lovely, Lily." He murmured against her breast. "Your breasts are gorgeous and I love the way your nipples taste."

She blushed furiously. Barry had never been much of a talker in bed and he had never said anything even remotely suggestive to her. She was shocked to realize how much she liked it – how excited it made her. Judging by the sudden dampness that was flooding her panties, she more than just liked it.

"Are you wet, Lily?" His hot breath blew into her ear and she made a loud moan of excitement.

He moved his hand to her lower belly, rubbing the curve of it just above her pubic bone and she thrust her hips at him eagerly.

"Should I check for myself?" He sucked on her earlobe and she made a soft, pleading noise.

"Y-yes, please." She whispered.

He slipped his hand into her shorts and traced the waistband of her panties. "I bet you're soaking wet, Lily. I bet I could slide my cock into you easily."

"Logan!" She gave him a shocked look, mixed with desire, and he winked at her.

"Yes?"

"I – please touch me." She whispered.

"It would be my pleasure, Lily." He kissed her again and she ran her hands over his naked chest, threading her fingers through the coarse hair like she had dreamed of doing for weeks. He groaned when her fingers brushed against his flat nipple and she nipped his throat as he slid his hand into her panties. His fingers touched the soft curls and then suddenly he was pulling his hand free and pushing away from her. He yanked the covers up just as Hazel wandered into the room.

"Daddy?"

"Yeah?" He cleared his throat as Lily, her face burning, straightened her tank top under the covers.

"Is Lily awake?"

"I am." Lily sat up, holding the covers to her chest to hide her hard nipples, and smiled at Hazel. "Are you okay?"

"Yes. Will you make me French toast?" Hazel climbed on to the bed and stared curiously at Lily.

"Why is your face red, Lily?"

"I'm just a bit warm." Lily said quickly. She slid awkwardly out from under the covers and Hazel slid off the bed after her.

"Let me just go and get dressed and then we'll make some French toast, okay?"

"Okay. Can I come with you?"

"Uh, sure." She took Hazel's hand and led her from the bedroom without looking at Logan.

Logan groaned and flopped back on the bed, looking up at the ceiling. What the hell just happened? He rubbed his forehead and said a silent prayer that Lily wouldn't just up and quit before he had the chance to apologize.

* * *

"Lily? Could we talk for a minute?" Logan stood in the doorway of the kitchen and stared worriedly at her. She hadn't eaten anything at breakfast and she wouldn't look him in the eye. Hazel was playing in the living room and he glanced quickly behind him, hoping she wouldn't choose this moment to join them in the kitchen.

"Lily?" She was standing at the counter with her back to him and he watched as she flinched and then turned around.

"I'm so sorry, Logan." She said hoarsely as she stared at the floor. "Please, don't fire me. I know how inappropriately I acted this morning and I have no excuse for it, but I swear I'll never do it again. Please, don't fire me."

"Lily, I'm not – "

She stared up at him, her eyes shiny with tears. "I'll find someplace else to stay when you're at home. You – you won't even have to see me. I'll just stay here when you're at work and – "

"Lily, stop!" He glanced behind him again. "I'm not going to fire you. In fact, I'm hoping that you won't quit. I – what happened this morning was my fault, not yours, and I wanted to apologize to you. I was the one who acted inappropriately and I wanted to, well, make it clear that I'm not expecting you to sleep with me. I hired you to be Hazel's nanny, not my uh, bed mate, and I shouldn't have done or said what I did this morning."

She didn't reply and he rubbed at his beard nervously. "I'll understand completely if you tell me to take this job and shove it up my ass, but you have my word that what happened this morning will never happen again. I would really hate for Hazel to lose you because I couldn't keep my hands to myself."

She wiped at the tears that were sliding down her cheeks. "I'm not going to quit." She whispered.

He nodded with relief. "Thank you. And you don't need to find someplace else to stay during your time off, unless it would make you feel better. But again, I promise I won't touch you like that ever again."

A strange look crossed her face before she nodded. "Thank you, Logan. I appreciate that. And I'm sorry too." She paused and blushed furiously. "I kissed you first so this really is my fault but I swear I'm not a – a sex maniac, or anything like that."

He grinned, he couldn't help it, and the red deepened in her cheeks. "I know you're not, Lily. So, we're good then? Everything's back to normal and still friends?" He stepped towards her, holding his hand out.

She shook it a bit gingerly and gave him a tentative smile. "Yes, still friends."

"Great." He left the kitchen and Lily took a shuddering breath.

She was so relieved that he wasn't going to fire her that she felt nearly weak with it. She brushed her hand across her face, not surprised that it was trembling, and stared out the window. He wanted things back to normal and she did too so everything was good. Of course, if that was true, why was she feeling a weird sense of disappointment that he had so quickly and eagerly promised to never touch her like that again?

She stared down at her large belly and shook her head. She was an idiot. She was eight months pregnant and even if she hadn't been, someone like Logan would never find someone like her attractive. She knew she wasn't ugly like Barry had so often told her, but she was far from pretty.

He said you were lovely.

A sweet hot rush of pleasure went through her as she remembered what else he had whispered to her in his bed. She glanced at her breasts, not surprised to see the nipples hard and poking through her plain cotton bra.

She swallowed and pushed the memory of Logan's deep voice out of her head. His wife just died six months ago. No doubt he was lonely, and he had been half-asleep when she had started kissing him. He probably reacted out of instinct and –

"Lily?"

She turned and smiled at Hazel. "Yeah, honey?"

"Come play with me."

"Alright." She took the little girl's hand and followed her out of the kitchen.

Chapter 8

Lily closed the door to Hazel's room and moved quietly down the hall. Hazel had woken this morning with a slight fever and she had been whiny and in a bad mood. She had just poked at her food at lunch, and afterwards Lily had given her some Children's Tylenol and cuddled with her on Hazel's bed until she had fallen asleep.

She hesitated outside the door of the spare bedroom. She was feeling lonely and bored and after a moment, she opened the door and went in. She had never been in this room and she glanced around curiously. There was a piece of gym equipment in the left corner, free weights piled around it, and a desk, its surface piled with mail and random pieces of paper, was under the window. She smiled a little. Logan was messy. It was a stark contrast to Barry's almost compulsively neat behaviour, and she had to admit that she found it a bit adorable.

There was a bookshelf along one wall, crammed full of books and binders and she studied the books on the shelf, her fingers trailing absentmindedly along the spines. There was a photo album stuffed between two large books on home repair and she glanced around a bit guiltily before pulling it free.

She sat down in the office chair and flipped the album open. Her breath caught in her throat. There were pictures of Logan with a stunningly beautiful blonde woman and she didn't need to see the strong resemblance to Hazel to know that it was Erin. She turned the pages, studying each picture carefully.

They looked happy, she mused. There were lots of pictures of the two of them and she was a little surprised at how much younger and carefree Logan looked. She traced a picture of him standing in front of the fire station with Rob before turning the page.

She frowned a little. These pictures had obviously been taken a few years later. Logan had a beard, and Erin's hair was longer and she was much thinner. Her previous good looks had faded a bit. Her cheekbones jutted out and while Logan was grinning into the camera, she had a look of solemn sadness.

Lily flipped through the pages. She stopped when she saw the picture of a hugely-pregnant Erin. She had filled out with the pregnancy and she looked much healthier but she had that same look of sadness on her face. Logan was standing beside her, his hands folded behind his back, and Lily found it odd that they weren't touching. Logan had said that Erin didn't like her belly touched while she was pregnant but she wondered why they didn't have their arms around each other like in the earlier photos.

She glanced down at her own large belly. She didn't have a single picture of herself pregnant and she made the sudden decision to ask Janet to take some pictures of her. She had found out over their frequent coffee dates that Janet was an amateur photographer, and she was confident that Janet would snap a few pictures for her.

She continued to turn the pages, her face lighting up when she found the pictures of Hazel as a baby. The little girl had been a bit funny looking, her face squished and her blonde hair sticking up like porcupine quills, but Lily thought she was beautiful. She caught her breath at the picture of Logan holding her. His face beamed with happiness and pride, and she blinked rapidly as her throat tightened and tears threatened. It was obvious how much Logan loved Hazel, and she felt a moment of sadness that her baby would never know what it was like to have a father who loved her like that.

On the next page there was a picture of Erin holding Hazel. Hazel looked to be about two or three and Lily stared in horror at Erin. Her good looks had completely faded. Her blonde hair was dull and lifeless, and there were small scabs and marks on her face and arms. She was staring down at Hazel but Lily saw no love in her eyes, just a terrible emptiness that brought goose bumps to her arms.

She shut the photo album abruptly and carried it back to the bookshelf. She couldn't stand to look at the pictures anymore. Something terrible had obviously happened to Erin, something so awful that neither Logan nor Hazel would talk about it, and her heart was hurting for both of them.

She shoved the album back into its place and left the room, shutting the door quietly behind her. She was curious about what had happened and why Logan didn't seem to miss his wife, but she couldn't bring herself to ask him about it. Although it had been a week since she had woken in his bed, things still felt a bit awkward between them and she could only imagine the look on his face if she asked him why he didn't miss his dead wife.

She limped down the stairs to the kitchen. She would have a cup of tea and wait for Hazel to wake up. If she still wasn't feeling better, she'd text Logan and ask him if she should make a doctor's appointment for her.

* * *

"What are you doing, Lily?" Hazel asked curiously as she and Logan joined her in the baby section.

It was two days later. Hazel was feeling much better and when she found out that Lily was going shopping, she had asked to come along. Lily had agreed and was secretly thrilled when Logan tagged along with them.

"I'm just writing some prices down." Lily smiled at the little girl before quickly writing the price down of the stroller in a small green notebook. Logan peered over her shoulder at the notebook. He could see a list of baby items with the price written beside them in Lily's neat handwriting.

"Why?" Hazel asked.

"Oh, I just want to get some idea of the price of stuff so I can make a budget for the baby supplies." Lily explained. She placed the notebook in the top section of the buggy and watched as Hazel touched the stroller.

"This is nice."

"It is." Lily agreed. She bit her bottom lip in thought. The stroller, as well as most of the larger items on her list, was way over her budget. Unfortunately those types of big ticket items were few and far between in the thrift stores and if they were there they were old and, she suspected, not up to current safety standards. She would have to borrow Logan's iPad and check out the online classifieds. People were always selling baby stuff. Maybe she would get lucky and find some good quality items within her price range.

She smiled at Logan and Hazel before wandering down the aisle. She traced the small bathtub meant to be placed in the sink and picked up the notebook before hesitating and placing it back in the buggy. She didn't need a bathtub specifically for the baby. She could just wash her in the kitchen sink. That's what her mom did with her.

"Are you buying anything today?" Logan's deep voice sent a small, sweet shiver down her spine. She had dreamt about him last night. Had dreamed that she was in his bed and straddling him. His warm hands had stroked her round belly and he had smiled up at her when she had slid his large, hard cock into her aching, wet core. The dream had been so realistic she nearly cried with frustration when she had woken before she could find her release.

She sighed angrily. She had assured Logan multiple times that she wasn't a sex maniac but she was starting to doubt her claim. Over the last week or so, all she could think about was sleeping with him. How it would feel to have him take her while he whispered hot and naughty things in her ear and his large hands stroked and kneaded her breasts.

She had never been so horny in her entire life. She was sure of it. Despite her huge belly, despite her swollen ankles and miserably sore back, she was almost desperate to have Logan between her legs. Her core ached all the time now, a deep and pulsing ache that could only be taken away by Logan. She could hardly stop herself from touching him, from begging him to kiss her and touch her and –

"Lily?"

She twitched when she felt his hand on her shoulder and he immediately pulled it away. "I'm sorry."

"It's fine." She gave him a weak smile. "I was um, woolgathering. What did you say?"

"I asked if you were going to buy anything today." He pointed at her notebook. "You have a pretty big list."

"Oh, um, right. I'm going to pick up some diapers and some other small things today." She smiled at him.

"Are you buying the playpen and stroller?"

"Not today. I'm going to keep my eye out for a better deal." She said nervously.

He nodded but didn't reply and she gave him another tentative smile before walking away.

* * *

"I like this one!" Hazel squeaked excitedly.

Logan popped his head into the living room. He had been upstairs working out and his shirt was damp with sweat and sticking to his wide shoulders.

"Did I hear Janet?"

Lily looked up from where she was sitting on the couch with Hazel. "Yes. She just stopped by for a moment."

"What are you looking at?"

"Pictures, daddy!" Hazel pointed to the spot beside Lily. "Sit down and look at them with us."

"Sure." He said agreeably. He sat down next to Lily, being careful not to let his thigh brush against hers.

"I asked Janet to take some maternity pictures." Lily explained. "She came by a couple days ago while you were working and we had a little photo shoot. Didn't we, Hazel?"

Hazel nodded and Lily stroked her soft hair. "I asked her to pick her favourite ones and put them on a CD for me but she went above and beyond. She had a bunch of the pictures developed and put them in this photo album. Wasn't that nice of her?"

"Very nice." Logan smiled at her and her stomach did a lazy flip flop.

"Anyway, she just stopped by on her way to yoga to drop them off." Lily continued.

"Well, let's take a look at them." Logan said.

Suddenly feeling nervous, Lily flipped back to the first page of the album as Logan peered down at them. She turned the pages, her smile growing larger as she stared at the pictures.

"She did a great job." Logan commented.

"She really did." Lily couldn't believe how good the pictures were. Janet had instructed her how to pose and although it had felt awkward and unnatural at the time, the pictures showed no sign of it. She looked happy and content and almost pretty, she thought.

She turned the page and heard Logan's sharp inhale. Hazel had been eager to be a part of the photo shoot, and Janet had shot a number of pictures with Hazel touching and kissing Lily's belly. She had printed them in both colour and black and white, and Lily stared stunned at them. They had turned out gorgeous and she reached out and traced Hazel's sweet face before glancing at Logan.

He had a weird look on his face and a thread of worry shot through her. She hadn't asked Logan if she could take pictures with Hazel and she wondered if he was angry. "Logan, I'm sorry. I should have asked your permission first but I didn't even think about it. Hazel really wanted to be in the pictures, and Janet thought it was a great idea so I – "

"These are beautiful." He interrupted her. "I'm glad you took some with Hazel." He stared at the picture of Hazel standing in front of Lily. Lily's shirt was lifted and Hazel had her small hands flat on her bare, swollen belly. She was grinning up at Lily and Lily, her face flushed with happiness, was smiling down at her.

"I – do you think I could have a copy of this one?" He asked suddenly.

She nodded. "Oh sure, of course. It's a really sweet picture of Hazel."

"Yeah." He cleared his throat. It was a sweet picture of Hazel but he would be stupid to try and deny that Hazel was the only reason he wanted a copy of it. Lily had never looked more beautiful and he was anxious to have a picture of that moment Janet had captured so effortlessly.

"I'm pretty." Hazel announced suddenly.

Lily laughed. "Yes you are, honey."

"Do you think I'm pretty, daddy?" Hazel asked.

"You're the prettiest girl I know." Logan reached across Lily and tickled Hazel lightly. She giggled before reaching down and turning the page on the photo album.

All of the spit in Logan's mouth dried up and he stared mutely at the photo of Lily. His pulse was roaring in his ears and he made an unintelligible croaking noise when he heard Hazel speaking to him.

Lily gave him an embarrassed look. As usual, her face was bright red and she hurried to flip the page in the album.

"I'm looking at it!" Hazel protested immediately and pushed the page back.

Lily stared at Logan. He was studying the black and white photo and she could see a red flush creeping up his neck.

"Janet wanted to do some uh, more artsy types of pictures." She said weakly. She looked at the photo again, wondering what Logan was thinking.

Logan reminded himself to breathe as he stared at the picture of Lily. She was standing in front of the window in his bedroom, wearing one of his white collared shirts and a pair of tiny white panties. His shirt was unbuttoned and although it was draped in a way that hid the majority of her breasts, he could still see the curve of her left one and just a hint of her pink nipple. His shirt fell to her knees and Janet had posed her so that her right thigh hid the scar on her left one.

She looked perfect and beautiful. Her dark hair was straight and smooth and flowing down her back. One hand rested gently on her stomach while the other held back the curtain at his window so she could look outside. The light from the window was perfect, it bathed Lily in a warm glow, and Janet had captured a look of soft contentment on her face.

His eyes drifted to her bare belly and then back to her nearly-naked breasts and that hint of nipple. He studied it, remembering how it had felt to suck on her tight, swollen nipples, and looked away in a hurry. Seeing Lily mostly naked in his shirt was going to give him a goddamn erection.

"I'm sorry, Logan." Lily whispered.

"For what?" He asked hoarsely as he studied his own knees. He wondered just how creepy he would sound if he asked Lily for a copy of this picture too. Pretty damn creepy, he decided.

"I should have asked if we could use your bedroom for pictures and your, uh, shirt. It was Janet's idea but I liked the idea and wanted to do it. I washed your shirt afterwards." She finished lamely.

He shook his head. "It's fine. You didn't need to ask my permission." He continued to stare at his knees, willing his cock to behave itself, as Hazel leaned against Lily's leg.

"I think you look pretty, Lily."

"Thank you, honey." Lily replied softly.

"Do you think Lily is pretty, daddy?" Hazel asked.

There was an awkward silence and Lily could almost feel her cheeks catching on fire.

"Yes, Hazel. I do." Logan finally said.

"But not as pretty as me." Hazel replied confidently.

Lily burst out giggling and the moment of awkwardness passed. Logan winked at her. "You'll always be the prettiest girl I know, baby bug."

Hazel grinned and then laughed when Lily's belly twitched. She pressed her hand against Lily's belly. "Hi baby!"

She reached for Logan's hand. "Daddy, the baby's kicking!" She pressed his hand to Lily's belly.

Logan knew he should be pulling his hand away but the feel of Lily's baby moving under his hand filled him with the same wonderment as before. He couldn't help but press his hand more firmly against her, anxious to feel the next kick.

"Hi baby." He echoed Hazel's words and grinned foolishly at Lily's belly when the baby kicked in response.

"She knows our voices!" Hazel laughed. She squealed loudly when the baby kicked even harder.

"I think you're right!" Logan couldn't hide the excitement in his voice and he leaned closer to Lily's belly as he began to rub it gently. "Hi baby girl. Is our sweet baby having a good time in there? Does she recognize her daddy's – "

He stopped and glanced up at Lily, praying like hell she hadn't heard what he just said. The look on her face suggested she had heard perfectly and, embarrassed beyond belief, he stood up abruptly.

"I'm going to go take a shower." He nearly ran from the room.

* * *

Lily hung her jacket in the front closet before taking her boots off. She had gone to a matinee with Janet and her two oldest, and her back was aching miserably from sitting in the theatre seat.

She rubbed it as she hauled her body up the stairs. Her back was aching and her leg was hurting and she wanted to climb into a hot bath and soak forever. The house was quiet. Logan's truck was in the garage but she suspected that he had taken Hazel for a walk to the park. Spring had finally arrived and although it was a bit wet and mucky out, the sun shone warmly and flowers were starting to sprout out of garden beds across the neighbourhood.

She limped wearily down the hall towards her bedroom. She would have her hot bath and go to bed early tonight. She might even ask Logan if he had a hot water bottle to rest against her back. It would help –

Her mouth dropped open and she stared in shock at her bedroom.

"Surprise!" Hazel shouted.

She was standing in Lily's bedroom and holding a screwdriver as Logan placed the mattress in the crib pushed against the wall. The floor was covered in boxes and, she realized mutely, a bassinet, playpen, stroller, swing and various other baby items.

"What? Where did this stuff come from?" She whispered as Hazel ran over and wrapped her arms around Lily's belly.

"It was my stuff when I was a baby!" She crowed excitedly. "Daddy brought it out of the attic."

"Logan?" She blinked at him as he walked over and stood beside her.

"I kept all of Hazel's baby stuff and I figured maybe you could use it. There are clothes and blankets and baby toys."

He pointed to the bassinet sitting beside the bed. "I though the baby would like an actual bassinet more than a, you know, laundry basket."

She didn't reply and he cleared his throat. "We'll probably need to buy a new stroller and car seat but you can choose to use whatever you want. I mean, you don't have to use any of it if you don't want to. I just thought it might be a bit cheaper and easier for you."

She threw her arms around him and hugged him tightly. "Oh, Logan. Thank you! Thank you so much!" She whispered into his ear. "I – I'll use all of it. It's perfect!"

He put his arms around her and hugged her back, relishing the feel of her small body against his. It was the first time she had touched him since that morning in his bed, and he hadn't realized how much he had missed even her innocent, friendly touches.

When she tried to step back, he squeezed her tighter and held on. He didn't know when she would touch him again and he wanted just a few more minutes. She didn't protest. In fact, she relaxed against him and rested her head on his broad chest.

He hesitated and then tentatively rubbed her lower back. Erin hadn't let him touch her very much during her pregnancy but he could still remember how sore her back had been. Lily groaned and nearly sank into his embrace. She made a soft moan of approval when his hands slipped under her shirt and he rubbed and kneaded her bare skin. He moved one arm around her bottom and hips, holding her firmly, and continued to rub her lower back with the other. She was leaning against him like a boneless kitten, resting her entire weight against him, and he knew if he let go of her she would simply fall over.

"Does that feel good, Lily?" He asked huskily.

"Mmm, so good." She murmured. "My back is really sore."

He moved his hand higher, sliding it under her bra to stroke her middle and upper back. She arched into him, pressing her breasts and belly against him, and made another soft moan of delight.

He returned his hand to her lower back, rubbing and stroking her soft flesh, as he glanced around the room. Hazel had wandered away to one of the boxes. Her back was to them and she was digging through the toys, glancing curiously at them as she set them on the carpet.

He slipped his hand inside the waistband of Lily's yoga pants and rubbed just above her ass. She sighed and moved her hands restlessly against his back. Taking a deep breath, feeling his cock hardening in his pants, he slipped his hand completely inside her pants and panties and cupped her ass cheek in his hand. It was both soft and delightfully firm, and he squeezed it roughly as she made a quiet, gasping moan and her fingers dug into his back.

He rubbed and kneaded her entire ass, his blood heating up at the way her pelvis jerked against him in response.

He took another quick look in Hazel's direction as Lily lifted her head and pressed her face into his thick neck. He nearly groaned out loud at the feel of her soft tongue licking the rough stubble.

His hand moved lower and he pressed his fingers against the back of her tightly-closed thighs. She parted them immediately and he traced them lightly before sliding his fingers between her legs. It was a bit awkward. Lily's belly was in the way and she was so short he had to hunch over her, but he was determined to feel her warmth. He had an undeniable urge to see if she was wet, to know if she was as turned on as he was, and he bit back the loud groan when his fingers slid easily over the wet lips of her pussy.

She shuddered against him before lifting her head and pressing her mouth against his ear. "Please." She breathed.

Lust flamed within him. He wanted to carry Lily to his bedroom, pull off her clothing and put her on her hands and knees on his bed. He would lick her pussy until she came and then he would kneel behind her, slide his cock into her warmth and find his own release. It had been a long time since he'd been with a woman, and Lily was so soft and warm and –

"Daddy?"

He had pulled his hand out from Lily's pants and stepped away from her before Hazel had even turned. He whipped around and stared at the crib.

"Yeah, Hazel?"

"Can I keep this toy? I like it." He looked over his shoulder. Hazel was holding out a stuffed bear and giving him a pleading look.

"Of course you can, honey." Lily, her face flushed and her voice unsteady, limped over to the bed. She sat down on it and, without looking at Logan, began to go through one of the boxes that was sitting on it.

"Oh, this is so sweet." She gave Hazel a faint smile and held up a tiny yellow dress as Logan smoothed his t-shirt and headed for the door.

"Where are you going?" Hazel called.

"Just to grab a drink. I'll be back in a bit." He disappeared out the door as Hazel climbed on to the bed beside Lily.

"Did we surprise you, Lily?" She asked eagerly.

"You sure did. I love that the baby will get to wear your baby clothes, Hazel. That makes me very happy." Lily smiled at her.

"Me too." Hazel replied.

Chapter 9

Lily walked carefully down the dark stairs. Her back was hurting so much she could hardly sleep and she had terrible heartburn. She had gone to bed early but had tossed and turned restlessly until finally giving up and crawling out of bed.

She sighed as she stepped off the last stair. She and Logan had, by unspoken agreement, not talked about what happened in her bedroom yesterday. She pushed her hair out of her face as she walked down the dark hallway. She couldn't believe she had allowed Logan to touch her so intimately in front of Hazel. Her face burned and she said a silent prayer of thanks that Hazel hadn't seen anything. She was being a terrible nanny. Not only was she throwing herself at her employer but she was doing it in front of his child. She –

She paused at the doorway of the living room, squinting in to the darkness when a dull flash of light caught her eye. It took a moment for her to realize it was Logan, sitting in the dark and drinking from a bottle of what looked like whiskey.

She hesitated as he tipped the bottle and took another long swallow. He had been acting weird all day but she had chalked it up to what happened yesterday and just tried to stay out of his way. She sighed. She needed to speak to him, obviously. She would apologize and beg for her job yet again.

"Logan?" She stepped into the room and rubbed her hands nervously over her shorts.

"It's late. Why are you up?" He asked.

She shrugged. "I couldn't sleep."

"Me either." He took another drink of whiskey before holding the bottle out to her. "Want a drink?"

"Uh – "

"Oh wait – that's not right. You can't drink." He shook his head and snorted soft laughter. "Jesus, I'm a fucking genius."

She sat down beside him on the couch. "Logan, are you – are you alright?"

"Just fine. Why?" He grinned widely at her.

"Well, I've never seen you drink anything stronger than a beer before."

"I'm not much of a drinker." He admitted. "I like to treat my body as a temple." He slapped his flat stomach and winked at her.

She smiled a little. "Okay, Logan. Whatever you say."

"Yeah, whatever I say." He muttered and took another long drink of whiskey.

"Logan? Do you – "

"Today is Erin's birthday." He said abruptly. "Hazel doesn't remember and I didn't tell her. Does that make me a horrible dad?"

She reached out and patted his hand timidly. "No. I don't think so. I'm sorry, Logan. I know you must miss her."

He snorted. "Yeah, I miss her about as much as you miss your husband."

"What – what do you mean?" She whispered.

He gave her a dry look. "You never talk about him, you have no pictures of him anywhere in your room and you're not wearing your wedding ring. Look me in the eye and tell me you miss your husband, and I'll eat this pillow." He pointed to the pillow on the couch.

"What happened to your wife?" She whispered.

He sighed and took another drink of whiskey. "Tell me why you don't miss your dead husband and I'll tell you what happened to Erin."

She hesitated and then sat back on the couch, tucking her feet up under her and shoving a pillow behind her to support her aching back. "After my parents died I was just lost, you know? I didn't know what to do or where to go. I had been dating Barry for a few months and he was really good to me when they died. He helped me with their funerals and all the horrible things you have to take care of when your loved ones die. When he asked me to marry him, I said yes without even really thinking about it."

She stared at her hands. "After we got married, he changed. Barry was, well, he was abusive."

Logan stiffened beside her, his hand tightening around the bottle of whiskey. "He hit you?"

She shook her head. "No, he never laid a hand on me. He was more emotionally abusive I guess you could say. He used to tell me I wasn't very pretty and that I would never do better than him. He thought I was dumb and he hated my cooking and how I kept the house. He didn't want me to get a job, said my job was to take care of him, and I went along with it. I never had many aspirations for a career, you know? I just always wanted to be a wife and mom."

She rubbed her round belly. "At first I use to argue with him. I used to tell him he was wrong and that I wasn't as awful as he said. But after a while it just got – got easier to let him say those horrible things. And then I slowly started to believe them."

Logan stared at the bottle in his hand. That explained why Lily was so timid and unsure about everything she said and did. "They aren't true." He said abruptly. "Those things he said – they're not true, Lily."

"Yeah, I know." She sighed. "Anyway, the night of the car accident I was sitting in the passenger seat listening to Barry rant and rave about how terrible I was, and I just knew I couldn't stay with him any longer. I didn't love him. I had stopped loving him years ago. Once I found out I was pregnant I couldn't stop wondering if Barry would say the same horrible things to our child. I – I didn't want to give up on my marriage, but I didn't want our baby growing up and hearing her dad say awful things about her mom or about her. Do you understand?" She asked pleadingly.

"I do." He nodded.

"I told Barry I wanted a divorce and he freaked out and told me that the marriage was over only when he said it was. And then we got in the car accident and he died and I was free. He never even knew about the baby." She said quietly.

"He left everything to his parents?" He asked.

"Yes. I like to think of it as Barry's final 'fuck you'." She laughed bitterly.

He twitched a little. He has never heard Lily curse before and it sounded strange coming from her sweet mouth.

She stared at her hands and wondered if she should tell him about Barry's parents offer to buy the baby. Before she could decide, he took another swig of whiskey and sighed loudly.

"Erin was a drug addict. When I met her she had only been sober for a couple of months. She was still fragile and weak, and I was drawn to that. Rob says I have a white knight complex."

She didn't reply and he took another drink. "We married pretty quickly and about a year after, she started using again. I figured it out almost immediately and got her into rehab. She didn't want to go but I made her. She got clean and a month later she got pregnant with Hazel. I watched her like a hawk during the pregnancy. I was terrified that she would use while she was pregnant. She swore she wouldn't and she didn't, but my continual suspicion wore on her. She was pretty unhappy with me, to put it mildly, and we fought constantly during her pregnancy."

He sighed and stared into the darkness. "Once Hazel was born I thought things would get better but Erin never really bonded with her. I wouldn't admit it at the time but all Erin really cared about was the drugs. She started smoking pot when Hazel was about a year old. She tried to hide it from me, but I knew. Over the next couple of years she started smoking more and more, and eventually she went back to the hard drugs."

He drained the bottle and dropped it to the floor beside him. "I took a leave from work and tried to convince Erin to go back into rehab. She refused. I should have kicked her out but I thought Hazel needed a mom, even a bad one like Erin, and I thought I could still save her. I was convinced that if I just tried a little harder, I could fix her. It wasn't for me. I couldn't even pretend by then that I still loved her but I wanted Hazel to have her mom. I was a fool."

"No you weren't." She whispered. She reached out and touched his hand and he grabbed her hand with a panicky tightness, linking their fingers together.

"The night that Erin died, I had gone to the store. Hazel had a bit of a cold and we had run out of cough medicine. Erin actually seemed pretty normal that night. She hadn't done meth for a couple of days and she had told me she was trying to get clean. I wasn't going to be gone long and Hazel was sleeping on the couch so I decided to leave her with Erin."

He swallowed thickly. "I was only gone twenty minutes at the most but when I got home, Erin was dead on the floor with a needle in her arm and Hazel was sitting in the corner. She was rocking back and forth and staring at Erin. She – she watched her own mother overdose and die."

"Oh, Logan." Lily whispered. She slid over and put her arm around his broad shoulders. He turned and hugged her tightly, burying his face in her neck as she stroked his hair and the back of his neck. "I'm so sorry."

"It was my fault. I shouldn't have let Erin stay. I shouldn't have believed that I could fix her and I should never have left Hazel with her that night. Hazel was traumatized and I was so afraid that she would never – never speak again."

His voice was cracking and she held him more tightly, planting small kisses on his temple. "She seems fine now. She's still in therapy and the therapist believes Hazel is doing really well. You can't blame yourself for what Erin did. Alright?"

He shrugged before he leaned back and stared at her. "Thank you, Lily."

"For what?"

"For being so good to Hazel. You're the reason she's talking again, the reason she's – she's acting normal and happy and I can never repay you for that."

Lily shook her head. "You're giving me too much credit, Logan. Hazel just needed time, that's all."

He frowned. "No, I don't believe that. I don't believe that at all."

His gaze dropped to her mouth and she felt a trickle of desire in her belly. She berated herself silently. Now was not the time to let her libido call the shots.

"You're so pretty, Lily." Logan whispered. He rubbed his thumb across her lower lip and she moaned shakily before scooting backwards on the couch.

"You've had a bit too much to drink, Logan. I think it's time you went to bed."

He didn't answer and she stood up and held her hand out. "Come on. I'll help you upstairs."

He took her hand and she led him up the stairs and into his room. "Climb into bed, Logan."

He shook his head. "I have to get undressed first."

"Right." She said nervously. She watched him hop around on one foot as he tried to pull his sock off and bit back the soft giggle when he cursed and fell on to the bed.

"Here." She pulled first one sock off and then the other as he reclined on the bed, before patting his leg. "Sit up, honey."

He sat up and lifted his arms so she could pull his t-shirt off. She stared at his chest, her mouth going dry with lust, and he grinned at her and stood up. He weaved unsteadily and she put one hand on his chest to steady him.

"I like it when you touch me, Lily." He said softly. "I know it isn't appropriate but I think about touching you all the time. Do you think about touching me?"

"Yes." She whispered.

"You should join me in my bed." He stroked her bare upper arm and she shivered with need.

He leaned down until his warm breath washed over her. "Let me make you feel good, Lily."

She sighed. The scent of whiskey was all around them and she knew Logan was drunk. He didn't know what he was saying and she wouldn't take advantage of that, no matter how badly she wanted him.

"I think you should crawl into bed and get some sleep, Logan." She said firmly. "Take your pants off."

"You take my pants off." He gave her a look that reminded her so much of Hazel when she was pouting, that she couldn't stop the giggle.

"What?" He was running his fingers back and forth over her collarbone and she lightly pushed them away. He dropped his hands to her belly and began to rub it instead.

"Nothing." She quickly unbuttoned and unzipped his jeans and pushed them down his legs. His thighs were heavily muscled and she resisted the temptation to touch them as he stepped out of his pants.

He was still rubbing her belly and she pushed on his chest. "Get into bed, Logan."

He sat down on the side of the bed and before she could stop him, he had lifted her night shirt and kissed her bare belly just above her navel. She shivered and ran her fingers through his hair as he placed soft kisses across her swollen belly.

"Hi baby girl." He said loudly as he stroked her belly. The baby kicked and Logan gave her a delighted grin.

"She really does recognize my voice, doesn't she?"

"Yes, I think so." Lily smiled at him as he kissed her belly again.

"I can't wait to meet you, baby." He murmured against her belly. "I bet you'll be as pretty and sweet as your mama."

He rubbed and kissed her belly repeatedly, talking softly to the baby as Lily stroked his hair and blinked back the sudden tears. He glanced up at her and frowned. "Lily? Are you alright?"

"Yes, I'm good." She said hoarsely. "But you should get into bed. It's getting late."

"Yeah, I guess." He kissed her belly a final time. "Good night, baby."

She helped him crawl into the bed and tucked the covers around him. He blinked sleepily at her and yawned. "Good night, Lily."

"Good night, Logan." She stroked his forehead and crept quietly from his bedroom.

Chapter 10

"Do you want to know the real reason that Rob and I have five kids?"

Lily looked up from studying Logan's ass. He was bent over, rummaging through the cooler and she had been daydreaming about what it would be like to squeeze it. It was a beautiful spring day, the first day it felt like winter was actually over, and she was sitting in a lawn chair beside Janet at one of the town's parks. Nearly all of the employees from the fire station, along with their families, were there.

"It's a tradition." Logan had said as they cleaned up from dinner two nights ago. "We always have a spring barbeque and you have to come. Janet will be there."

"I'm not really family, Logan." She had protested weakly.

He had just grinned at her and refused to let her stay home.

Now, she smiled at Janet. "I would love to know the real reason why you and Rob have five children."

Her eyes drifted back to Logan. He was helping Rob lift the barbecue from the back of Rob's truck, and a shiver of need went through her as she watched the muscles in his back and arms flex and bulge with the effort.

"I get really horny when I'm pregnant."

Her eyes swung back to Janet in a hurry. "I'm sorry?"

Janet laughed. "I can't get enough of Rob when I'm pregnant. Not for the first three months. I spend those months dragging my sorry ass from the bed to the couch and eating nothing but toast and crackers, but once that stage is through?"

She wiggled her eyebrows at Lily. "I jump Rob every chance I get."

Lily blushed furiously and Janet laughed again. "It's true. Rob loves it when I'm knocked up. He gets laid at least once a day, sometimes twice."

Lily stared at the ground, her cheeks burning and her hands twisting in her lap. She wanted to hug Janet. Just hearing the woman admit that she craved sex during her pregnancy was making her feel better. She glanced up at her. "Thanks, Janet. I thought I was weird for uh, thinking about – you know."

Janet grinned. "I do know. Plus, it can't help living with Logan. That boy is gorgeous."

Lily gave her a wide-eyed look. "I'm not – not having sex with Logan."

"I know you're not." Janet said breezily. She leaned closer and studied first Logan and then Lily. "But the way you were staring at his ass earlier, makes me pretty confident that you'd like to. So why not go for it? Pregnancy sex is the best sex ever. I mean, it can be a bit awkward and you have to get creative with positions sometimes, but I swear – your orgasms are like a thousand times more intense. At least mine are."

Lily stared at her. She had never really participated in girl talk before and she could feel the embarrassment creeping through her. "I – Logan's my employer. It's not appropriate."

She hesitated. She wondered what Janet thought of the fact that she had only buried her husband five months ago and was now lusting after her employer. "My husband wasn't very nice to me." She said suddenly. "He um, he was emotionally abusive and I had asked him for a divorce before the car accident."

Janet reached over and squeezed her arm. "I'm glad you told me, honey. But I wasn't judging you for wanting Logan. I want you to know that."

"I know. I just – you know - didn't want you to think badly of me." Lily whispered.

"I don't. There's nothing wrong with being attracted to Logan. You know that, right?"

Lily shrugged. "I guess. It doesn't matter anyway. He doesn't feel that way about me."

Janet, taking a sip of tea from her thermos, coughed and choked. Lily thumped her on the back and gave her a look of alarm.

"Janet? Are you alright?"

"Just fine." Janet croaked. She cleared her throat. "Lily, I have never met a woman more in denial than you."

"I – I'm not in denial." She said weakly.

"Oh, of course you're not. Logan only thinks of you as Hazel's nanny, nothing more." She said the last in a whispered little mutter as the object of their conversation walked over.

"Lily? Are you too cold? Your jacket is pretty light. I could give you my sweater." He said anxiously.

She shook her head. "No, I'm fine. I don't – "

He was already stripping off his sweater and she smiled at him as he crouched beside her and carefully draped it over her legs and tucked it in under her thighs. "There, okay?"

"Yes, thank you."

"You're welcome." He said cheerfully. He rubbed her belly affectionately before straightening and heading over to Hazel. She was standing by the play equipment with the other children, and Lily heard her squeal with delight when Logan picked her up and tossed her into the air.

"Yeah, he doesn't think of you as anything but Hazel's nanny. That's obvious." Janet said sarcastically.

Before Lily could reply, Janet was standing and hugging a slender brunette. "Tammy! It's so good to see you, honey!"

"Thanks, Janet. I'm glad the guys invited me." The woman smiled at her and kissed her cheek.

"Of course they would. You'll always be part of our family, you know that." Janet squeezed the woman's arm and turned to Lily.

"Lily, this is Tammy Smith."

"Hi Tammy, it's nice to meet you." Lily started to struggle from her chair and Tammy held her hand out.

"Don't get up on my account." She said cheerfully. She sat in the empty lawn chair beside Lily and eyed her belly.

"So, how far along are you?" She asked politely.

"Only a few more weeks to go." Lily answered.

"Well, congratulations. I'm sure Logan must be thrilled. He's always loved kids."

"I'm not uh, with Logan. I'm just Hazel's nanny."

"Oh! I'm sorry. That was rude of me to just assume." Tammy gave her a look of embarrassment before glancing over at Logan. "So, you and Logan aren't dating?"

"No. I work for him." Lily said quickly.

"I see." She continued to stare at Logan, tapping her finger thoughtfully against one smooth cheek, before turning to Janet. "Has Logan dated anyone since Erin died?"

Janet shook her head. "No. I think he's focused on Hazel right now."

"That's a shame." Tammy replied. "He's a great catch." She stood up abruptly and smiled at the two women. "Could you excuse me? I think I'll go say hello to some of the guys."

Janet and Lily watched as Tammy made a beeline for Logan. Lily could feel her stomach tighten when Logan gave her a delighted look and hugged her tightly. She returned the hug, her hands lingering on the muscles of his arms before she crouched down and spoke to Hazel. Hazel hid her face in Logan's pants for a moment and Lily felt a brief moment of uncharacteristic smugness. Hazel loved her and –

She watched with disbelief as Tammy said something to Hazel and Hazel nodded before taking her hand. She allowed Tammy to lead her to the swings and she pushed the little girl gently back and forth as she talked animatedly to Logan.

"Uh oh." Janet sighed.

"What?"

"Tammy is – well, she's lonely. Her husband Ted was a firefighter in our unit. He died a couple of years ago."

"That's terrible. On the job?" Lily asked.

Janet shook her head. "No. He had cancer. Anyway, we still invite her to all the barbecues and functions, and I know the last year or so she's been actively getting back into the dating world. Which is good for her, it really is, but I should have known she would eventually go after Logan."

Lily swallowed the sudden blockage in her throat and stared down at her belly. Tammy was slender and gorgeous and Hazel already seemed to like her. Why wouldn't Logan be attracted to her? She certainly didn't have swollen ankles or a belly so big she couldn't see her own damn feet.

"Lily? Are you okay?" Janet asked kindly.

Lily nodded. "Yes. I – I think it's good if Logan can find someone. He deserves to be happy."

"Yes, he does." Janet said softly. "But Tammy is, well, she's a little damaged. She struggled with some issues before Ted died and I'm sure his death hasn't helped."

Lily shrugged. "Logan told me himself that he liked taking care of people, that he had a white knight complex. Sounds like Tammy might be the perfect person for him."

She winced inwardly at how petulant she sounded but Janet didn't seem to notice. "That he does. But you would think he learned his lesson after Erin. Has he told you about her yet?"

Lily nodded. "Yes. It must have been so awful for both him and Hazel."

"It was." Janet agreed. "It's nice to see him happy now." She glanced at Lily's belly. "Both he and Hazel are very happy."

Lily didn't reply. She was watching Logan again and a look of pinched worry crossed her face when Hazel took Tammy's hand and the three of them walked towards the other children. She sighed softly. Who Logan dated was none of her business and if Hazel liked Tammy, that was a good thing. She was happy for both of them.

* * *

"Lily! Guess what!" Hazel grabbed Lily's leg and stared excitedly at her.

"What, honey?"

"Tammy said she would take daddy and me to a movie and for dinner whenever I wanted."

"She did?" Lily arranged her face into what she hoped was a smile. "That's great!"

"Yep! I like her. She's nice."

"That's good, honey. I'm really glad." She stared down at her half-eaten burger and potato salad. What little appetite she had, had disappeared completely with Hazel's words and she set the plate down on the grass with a soft sigh.

"Did you get enough to eat, Hazel?" She asked.

"Yes. I'm going to go back to Daddy and Tammy now."

Without waiting for her reply, Hazel skipped away. Jealousy, strong and unpleasant, flowed through her and she rubbed her head wearily before lumbering to her feet. Her stomach was upset and she'd been having weird cramps off and on for most of the afternoon. She rubbed at her back before picking up her plate of half-eaten food and carrying it to one of the garbage cans.

"Lily? Are you alright?" Janet came hurrying up to her as she dumped her plate in the garbage.

"Yeah, I'm fine."

"You didn't eat very much."

"I'm not that hungry. My stomach is a bit upset." Lily grimaced and grabbed her side as another cramp rippled through her.

Janet frowned. "Are you having contractions?"

Lily blinked at her. "What? No, I can't be. I'm not due for another three weeks."

"Babies come early all the time, Lily." Janet replied.

Lily shook her head. "No, it isn't that. I was at the doctor just yesterday and the baby hadn't even turned into position yet. It's not contractions."

She winced as another cramp hit her and Janet rubbed her lower back. "False labour, maybe? Why don't you sit down for a bit?"

"Yeah, maybe I will. My back is killing me." She muttered.

Before Janet could lead her to a lawn chair, Logan was standing in front of her. "Lily?" He gave her an anxious look. "Are you okay? I saw you grab your stomach – is it the baby?"

He rested his hand on her stomach. "Are you going into labour?"

She shook her head. "No, I – "

"Rob! Get over here!" Logan shouted. Rob came hurrying over and Logan gave him a look of bright panic. "I think Lily's in labour."

"I'm not in labour." She said firmly. "I just have a few cramps."

"It might be false labour." Rob said.

"That's what I thought." Janet put her arm around Lily. "Come on, honey. Have a seat and – "

Logan tugged Lily away from Janet and lifted her into his arms. She gave a loud squeak of alarm and punched him on the shoulder. "Logan, put me down!"

"You're going to the hospital." He said as Hazel ran up to them and clung to his leg.

"Daddy? What's wrong?"

"Nothing's wrong, honey. Everything's fine." Logan said grimly. He was starting to sweat and Lily slapped him lightly on the shoulder again.

"Put me down, Logan. Please."

He frowned but did as she asked, keeping one arm firmly around her shoulders. "You need to go to the hospital. Tell her, Janet."

"It can't hurt." Janet said mildly.

Lily glared at her as Logan made a sound of triumph. "See? Janet's had five kids, she knows what she's talking about."

"Logan – "

"Janet, can you take Hazel for us? I'll pick her up after we – "

"I want to go with you and mommy!" Hazel whined.

Neither Lily nor Logan noticed the look that passed between Rob and Janet as Logan crouched next to Hazel. He gave her a distracted smile. "Honey, that's not a good idea. You'll have more fun with Aunt Janet and Uncle Rob then you will at the hospital."

"No!" Hazel pouted. "Please daddy, I want to go with you."

"That's fine, Hazel. You can come with us." Lily replied.

"Lily – "

"She can go with us, Logan. We won't be at the hospital for very long." She said determinedly. "I'm not in labour."

Chapter 11

Logan peeked into Lily's room. Like he suspected, Hazel was in Lily's bed with her tiny body plastered against Lily's back. They were both sleeping and he moved silently into the room and sat down gingerly on the side of the bed.

Lily was sleeping on her side and he reached out and smoothed a strand of her dark hair away from her face. She didn't move and after a moment he placed his hand on her belly and rubbed softly.

He studied her face carefully. She looked a bit tired and he supposed she was. They had been at the hospital for nearly four hours while they waited to see if the false labour would turn into actual labour. They had monitored the baby's heartbeat carefully and he had been thrilled when they had done an ultrasound just to be on the safe side. Lily hadn't asked him to leave while they did the ultrasound and he, with Hazel in his arms, had watched eagerly as the image of the baby came on the screen.

He had urged Lily to lie down when they got home and, rubbing her back, she had quickly agreed. It hadn't been ten minutes before Hazel had disappeared from the living room and he wasn't surprised to find her with Lily.

He continued to rub her belly and a small smile crossed his face when the baby kicked lightly. He leaned down and placed a soft kiss on her belly through her t-shirt. He loved touching her belly, loved feeling the baby kicking and moving, and he felt a moment of bitterness towards Erin for taking this joy away from him.

Lily twitched and he pulled his hand back guiltily. He needed to leave before she woke up and saw him sitting here rubbing her belly like a weirdo. He was already being too familiar with her, and if he wasn't careful she would quit on him. She might need the money but she didn't need her employer being all handsy with her. He needed to rein it in and control his need for her. It was his problem, not hers, that all he had to do was look at her now and he would get an erection. The poor woman was going to give birth any day and all he could think about was coaxing her into his bed.

He snorted softly and Lily's eyes popped open. She stared sleepily at him. "What's wrong?"

"Nothing." He said quickly. "I was just coming in to get Hazel. She snuck in here."

She twisted her head to look behind her. "Leave her. Her body heat feels good on my back."

He patted her leg gingerly. "How do you feel?"

"Good. No more cramps and my headache is gone."

"I'm glad. Are you hungry?"

"A little." She stretched as Hazel stirred behind her.

The little girl sat up, her blonde hair sticking up everywhere and pillow creases on her face. She blinked and then yawned hugely. "Hi, daddy."

"Hi honey. Are you hungry?"

"Yep."

"Why don't you and Lily rest for a little longer and I'll make us something to eat."

Hazel and Lily exchanged looks of such terror that Logan burst out laughing. "I'm not that bad of a cook."

Hazel looked up at the ceiling and Lily studiously examined her nails. Logan snickered. "Okay, fine. I'm that bad of a cook. I'll order us some pizza. How's that?"

"Yay!" Hazel flopped back on the bed. "I want pepperoni, daddy."

"Pepperoni it is." He leaned over Lily's legs and kissed Hazel's foot. Although he had just told himself he would stop touching her, he couldn't resist patting Lily's belly one last time before he stood and left the room.

* * *

Logan moved quietly through the dark house. He had to work at six tomorrow and it was already after midnight. He should have been in bed hours ago but he had felt restless and jumpy and hadn't bothered to even try sleeping.

He climbed the stairs and peered curiously at the bathroom door. Although it was late, the bathroom light was on and he could hear Lily's soft muttering. There was a loud banging noise that made him jump and he knocked softly on the door.

"Lily? Are you okay? Let me in."

"I'm fine. It's open." She snapped.

He opened the door. Lily was on her hands and knees with her upper half wedged into the cupboard below the sink. Various bathroom items were piled around her legs and he stared with more than a little passing interest at her upturned ass. She was wearing just a long t-shirt and it had risen up until he could see her ass clad in pale pink panties. His cock twitched and he pulled his shorts away from his crotch before clearing his throat.

"What are you doing?"

"I'm looking for a goddamn heating pad." Her voice was muffled but he could hear the irritation in it. "Do you not have one?"

"I don't think so."

She made a loud snort of anger and tried to wiggle free of the cupboard.

"Shit."

He crouched beside her. "What?"

"I'm stuck."

A wide grin crossed his face and he tamped down the laughter that was starting when her muffled voice said, "So help me God, if you laugh I will shove this curling iron up your ass."

"I'm not laughing." He said quickly.

"I can hear it in your voice, Logan Anderson." She said grouchily. "Are you going to get me out of here or not?"

He put his hands on her hips, eyeing her ass one final time, before pulling firmly. She popped out, cussing lightly and breathing heavily, and glared at him before muttering a thank you.

"You're welcome."

She shoved her shirt down, for once not blushing, and grabbed the top of the counter. She hesitated and then gave him an angry look. "Are you going to just stand there or help me up?"

"Sorry." He stood and then hooked his hands into her armpits and lifted her to her feet. She winced and grabbed at her back before sighing.

"Thank you. I'm sorry. I didn't mean to snap at you." She said moodily.

"That's alright. What's wrong?"

"My back hurts and I can't sleep because of it." She looked like she was about to cry. "I keep forgetting to buy a heating pad and I was hoping that you might have one. I decided to look and then I got stuck in the cupboard because I'm the size of a house."

Now she was starting to cry and she turned away, sniffing loudly, and grabbing for the tissue on the counter. "Sorry. Pregnancy hormones, I think."

"Here," he grabbed the bottle of lotion that was on the floor and took her hand, "come with me."

"What are you doing?" She asked as he tugged her towards her bedroom.

"You'll see."

He ushered her into her bedroom and towards the bed. He clicked the bedside lamp on and sat down on her bed, resting his back against the wall and spreading his legs. "Sit down with your back to me, Lily."

"Why?"

"Just trust me."

She sighed and climbed awkwardly between his legs. She crossed her legs and looked behind her. "What are you doing, Logan?"

He had filled his hand with lotion and he rubbed his hands together lightly. "Lift your shirt up a bit, Lily."

She lifted her shirt and made a loud moan of pleasure when Logan began to rub her lower back. She leaned forward, bowing her head and clasping her hands together as he rubbed and kneaded the lotion into her back.

"Oh my God." She moaned. "That feels so good."

"Good. I'll rub your back until you're sleepy, okay?" He replied.

"Yes. Thank you, Logan." She murmured.

He rubbed and stroked and kneaded her warm flesh for the next fifteen minutes. He tried to keep his thoughts strictly non-sexual but the feel of Lily's soft skin and her moans of pleasure were making his cock harden.

He moved his hands to her sides, stroking more lotion into her skin. Knowing he shouldn't, but not able to stop himself, he slid his hands to her belly. He rubbed the lotion across the tight skin, making sure to cover every inch of her belly with the smooth cream.

"That's feels wonderful, Logan." She moaned. She leaned back, resting her head on his chest as he rubbed her belly, and he wondered if she could feel his erection. If she could, she didn't acknowledge it and, after a moment, he put his mouth to her ear.

"You should take your shirt off, Lily. I don't want to get lotion all over it." He said hoarsely.

He waited for her to sit up and tell him to leave. Instead, she nodded and, with the same hoarseness in her voice, said, "That's a good idea."

She sat up and he helped her strip her shirt off. She dropped it to the floor and leaned back against him. Her soft hair tickled his throat and he forced himself to continue rubbing her belly as he stared down at her naked breasts. They were fuller than he remembered but her nipples were as pink and deliciously hard as the last time he had seen them.

He told himself not to touch. He told himself that Lily didn't need him manhandling her when she was nearly nine months pregnant, and then his hands were cupping her breasts and Lily was moaning and arching her back and he forgot every single reason why he shouldn't touch her.

He squeezed them gently, her nipples hard little pearls against his palms, and she made another breathless cry of need. He pulled lightly on her nipples, rolling them between his thumbs and fingers and she dug her hands into his thighs.

"Oh Logan." She moaned again.

He dipped his head and kissed her, sliding his tongue between her lips to lick and taste the sweet warmth of her mouth. She kissed him back eagerly, reaching up to stroke his beard as he massaged and caressed her breasts.

He sucked lightly on her tongue and she groaned and pressed herself against him. He pulled on her nipples and she arched her back again before nipping his bottom lip. He gasped and she gave him a nervous look.

"I'm sorry."

"Don't be sorry, sweetheart." He growled. "I love everything you do to me."

She smiled timidly at him and reached down to stroke his large thighs. "I want you, Logan."

"I want you too, Lily." He whispered. His right hand moved from her breast to her stomach. He caressed it lightly before following the curve of it to the waistband of her panties.

"Open your legs, sweetheart."

She spread her legs as he kissed her hard on the mouth. His hand slid under her panties and then he was touching her core, touching the hot and swollen flesh that had been aching for his touch for months, and she could barely stop herself from arching up off the bed.

"Oh my God." She moaned into his mouth. She reached behind her and wiggled her hand into his shorts. He groaned loudly when her fingers stroked along his shaft, and he thrust his pelvis against her.

"Jesus, Lily." He muttered.

She wrapped her fingers around him and squeezed lightly. "Is that – does that feel okay?"

"Better than okay." He whispered. "You're going to make me come if you keep touching me."

A hot rush of lust exploded within her and she began to stroke him roughly. He groaned and kissed her neck, sucking and licking at the sensitive skin as she stroked him back and forth. He pushed his fingers past the swollen lips of her pussy and rubbed at her clit.

Her hand tightened around him and she arched her hips upwards, moaning loudly. He rubbed at her clit, his cock swelling at her wetness.

"I love how wet you are, Lily." He whispered into her ear. He licked her earlobe and she whimpered with need. Her hand was stroking him faster in response to his touch and he realized that he was incredibly close to coming. He circled her clit, rubbing it firmly as his other hand cupped her breast and pinched her swollen nipple.

Her hand tightened almost painfully around him and he made a harsh low cry, rubbing her clit furiously as he came. Dimly he was aware of her slender body shaking against his as her orgasm shuddered through her, and he pulled her close as he fell back against the pillows, panting roughly. She collapsed against him, her chest heaving as her head lolled weakly on his chest. They stayed that way for a few minutes and then he gently pulled her hand out of his shorts.

"Lily? Are you okay?"

"Yeah." She murmured. "I'm great."

She yawned hugely and wiggled to her side, wrapping her arm around his waist and snuggling into him. "Sleepy." She muttered.

He smiled a little. She was practically asleep already and, moving slowly, he carefully eased out from under her and tucked her into the bed. She sighed and curled into a ball on her side, shoving her hand under her pillow and resting her other hand on top of her belly.

He leaned over her and placed a gentle kiss on her cheek as he rubbed her belly. "Good night, Lily."

She muttered something unintelligible and he kissed her again before quietly leaving her room.

Chapter 12

"So, you and Hazel had a good day?"

Lily stared at Logan's face on the screen of the iPad. He had called to face time with Hazel before bedtime, just like he always did, and after saying goodnight to her he had asked to speak to Lily.

She had left Hazel in her room, tucked into bed with a picture book, and carried the iPad to the living room.

"We did." She said quietly. "We went to the park for a bit and made peanut butter cookies this afternoon. They're in a container in the cupboard above the stove if you want some when you get home."

He smiled. "If there's any left in two days. Hazel loves peanut butter cookies."

"She does." She agreed.

There was an awkward silence and she watched on the screen as Logan cleared his throat nervously and glanced around.

"So, about last night..." He trailed off and took another look behind him.

Lily sighed. She had already decided she wouldn't beg for her job again. Although she knew what she had done with him last night was wrong, she wasn't going to apologize for it or beg him not to fire her. She had wanted him and, after the first good night sleep she'd had in weeks, she was actually feeling better and happier than she had in days.

That's your post orgasmic glow talking. A small voice whispered in her head.

She willed herself not to blush nor think about how she had spent a good portion of her day daydreaming about various schemes to get Logan back into her bed. That had been a useless waste of energy. From the look on Logan's face he was about to tell her just how much of a sex maniac he thought she was.

"I really enjoyed it." Logan said quietly.

She jerked in surprise. "You did?"

He nodded, his face a little red, and she smiled with relief. "Me too."

"Yeah?" He gave her his own look of surprise.

"Yes. And I um, just wanted to say thank you. The back rub and um," she could feel her face heating up but she carried on determinedly, "the other uh, thing really helped me sleep. I feel much better today than I have in a while."

He gave her a slightly naughty grin. "Any time you need help sleeping, Lily, just let me know. I'm more than happy to help."

She blushed furiously and he leaned closer to the screen, his voice warm and low. "Maybe when I get home, after

Hazel's in bed, I could show you other ways to help you sleep. I have plenty of ideas."

She swallowed as desire flamed in her core. "I – I'd like that, Logan."

"Me too." He said hoarsely. "All I've thought about all day was how you looked and sounded last night. How it felt when you came all over my –"

He stopped and faintly, Lily heard Rob's voice calling Logan's name. A look of frustration crossed his face before he gave her an apologetic smile. "I'm sorry. I have to go."

"Of course." She tried to act like she hadn't been about to come in her own pants just from the sound of his voice, and gave him a cheerful smile. "We'll talk to you tomorrow night, alright?"

"Yes. Good night, Lily."

"Good night, Logan."

* * *

Lily tucked the broom into the front hallway closet. She rubbed at her lower back for a moment and then winced when a spasm of pain went through it. It was late afternoon. Hazel had been grumpy and uncooperative for most of the day and when she had fallen asleep on Lily's bed half an hour ago, Lily had covered her with a quilt and let her sleep. The little girl had woken her with a nightmare just after midnight and the two of them had crawled into Logan's bed. Both she and Hazel had slept poorly and she was looking forward to when Logan got home tonight. Hazel would be all over him, she always was when he first came home, and Lily would have some alone time and a nice hot bath. She had slept terribly for the last three nights and she was hopeful that tonight she would sleep better.

You know you will. Especially if Logan's in your bed with all of his ideas on how to help you sleep.

She blushed, a little embarrassed by how excited the thought of Logan touching her, being inside of her, made her feel. Lusting after her employer was about the stupidest thing she could do but it was happening and it was useless to keep denying it. She wanted him and, despite her weird puffiness and huge belly, he wanted her too. It was shameful of her but she was going to enjoy it and take advantage of –

The doorbell rang, startling her, and she turned and limped to the front door. She opened it, her mouth dropping open at the two people standing nervously on the front step.

"Hello Lily."

She swallowed thickly. "What do you want?"

"We just want to talk. Please. Just talk – nothing more. I promise you." The tall, elegant grey-haired woman said pleadingly. "Will you let us come in?"

Lily sighed and the woman gave her husband a frantic look. "Please, Lily. Just hear us out. If you don't like what we have to say, we'll leave and never bother you again."

"Regina – "

"Hush, Charles!" The woman said immediately.

Charles, his face and demeanor so much like Barry's that Lily almost felt like she was looking at a ghost, nodded and folded his hands behind his back.

Regina gave Lily a hopeful look and with a soft sigh, she stepped back. "Come inside."

* * *

"How did you find me?" Lily sat down heavily in the chair across from the couch and stared at Barry's parents.

Regina sipped at the tea Lily had given her, the cup shaking minutely, and smiled tentatively at her. "We hired private detectives."

Lily looked at her in astonishment. "You're kidding me."

"We're not." Charles said quietly. "You're carrying our grandchild and you just left without letting us know where you were going. Did you think we would just accept that?"

"Charles!" Regina said warningly. "You promised."

"Sorry." He muttered. He glanced at Lily. "We were worried. You have no family and no money."

"Thanks to your son." Lily replied.

Regina winced. "What Barry did was wrong. We see that now, Lily."

"Do you? Or are you just anxious to get your hands on your grandchild?"

Regina shook her head. "No, that isn't it. We – we made a mistake in offering you the money in exchange for the baby. It's just – we were desperate to hang on to what little we had left of our son. The baby you're carrying is all we have left of our child."

Tears were forming in the woman's eyes and Lily could feel herself softening. In all the years she had known Regina, she had never once seen the woman cry. In fact, she had often thought privately that the woman was an emotionless robot.

Now, seeing her shaking and staring at the new lines on her face, she felt ashamed for what she had done. Barry had been terrible to her and Charles had never been much better, but Regina had always been polite if a little distant to her. She made herself harden her heart against them. These people had try to buy her baby from her and she would be wise to remember that.

"You tried to buy my baby. Why should I let you have anything to do with her?"

"Her?" Regina leaned forward eagerly. "You're having a girl?"

Lily nodded. "Yes."

"That's wonderful!" Regina's face had lit up with happiness and she reached out and squeezed Charles' hand. "We're going to have a granddaughter, Charles."

He nodded, his face a mask of barely-concealed emotion, and cleared his throat. "Have you picked out a name yet?"

Lily shook her head. "No."

Regina gave her a hesitant look. "The name Annabel has been in our family for generations. It was my grandmother's name, my mother's name and my middle name."

"It's very pretty." Lily said non-committedly.

Regina sank back in her seat. "We know what we've done is unforgiveable, Lily, but we're hoping you'll find it in your heart to forgive us. We want to be a part of her life."

Lily said nothing and Regina gave Charles a quiet look of despair. "We – we're hoping that you would let us help you with the baby. We know how expensive babies can be and we – "

"No." Lily said immediately. "I don't need or want your money."

Charles snorted. "You're working as a live-in nanny for a fireman. What are you going to do once the baby arrives? I doubt he'll be interested in keeping you on as a nanny once you have a newborn. What will you do for money then?"

"That's none of your business." Lily said tightly.

"None of our business? None of our business?" Charles' face was turning red and he sat forward on the couch. "You're carrying our son's child. It is absolutely our business! You have no right to – "

"Charles!" Regina nearly shouted his name and he stopped and gave her a look of anger. The woman neither relented nor shrank back and after a moment, he looked down at his lap.

"Sorry." He muttered.

"He really is." Regina said hurriedly. "The last few months have been very… difficult. We've been very worried about both you and the baby."

Lily gave her a look of disbelief and Regina nodded. "It's true, Lily. I know I haven't been the best mother-in-law and I'm sorry. I just – I'm not very good at expressing my emotions, but I've always liked you."

She glanced at Charles. "We – we know that Barry treated you badly and we appreciate that you stuck by him, that you stayed with him and loved him."

Lily felt a twinge of guilt go through her. She shook it off. Barry had been abusive and she had been right to want to leave him. "Your son was horrible to me."

"I know." Regina said softly. "I'm sorry for that."

"Yeah, I am too." Lily sighed.

There was a few moments of silence and then Regina gave her another timid smile. "Has everything gone well with the pregnancy?"

Lily nodded. "Yes. I haven't had any trouble."

"Good, that's really good." Regina said eagerly. "When are you due?"

"In another three weeks."

"That's coming up quickly." Regina smiled at her. "Do you – have you gotten everything prepared for her?"

"Yes."

"Do you need anything? We would love to help buy some of the bigger items. Maybe a stroller or a crib, if you need it."

Lily shook her head. "I have everything I need, but thank you."

"Well, if you think of something that you might need, don't hesitate to call us. We'd be more than – "

"Lily? Hazel? I'm home!" Logan's deep voice echoed down the hallway and Lily stood up nervously as he entered the living room.

"Hi!" He gave her a warm grin and stepped towards her. He hadn't noticed either Regina or Charles and she twitched nervously when he reached out and rubbed her belly. "How was your day? Where's Hazel?"

"She's having a nap. She had a nightmare and didn't sleep well last night."

He frowned. "Is she okay?"

"Yes. We talked about it today and she seems to be doing fine. She was a little on the grumpy side."

"How did you sleep?" He caressed her belly again and she caught his hand.

"Logan, I – "

"Have you been thinking about all the ways I can help – "

"Logan!" She said his name sharply and he gave her a curious look.

"What's wrong?"

"Logan, I'd like to introduce you to Charles and Regina Castro. Barry's parents."

His eyes widened and he turned to look at the couple sitting on the couch. His hand dropped to his side and Lily touched his arm gently as Charles and Regina stood up.

"Charles and Regina this is my employer, Logan Anderson."

"It's nice to meet you." Regina said politely as she held her hand out.

Logan stared at it and after an awkward moment, she let her hand drop.

"What are you doing here?" He asked bluntly.

Charles bristled. "What do you mean by that? She's carrying our grandchild. We have every right to be here."

"Every right? After what you did, you think you have every right to be in Lily's or her baby's life?" Logan said incredulously.

"Logan, don't – " Lily began nervously.

He gave her a confused look. Charles stepped closer and Logan moved protectively in front of her.

"Don't come near her."

Charles glared at him. "Who do you think you are?"

"I'm someone who cares about Lily. More than you two assholes do." Logan's face was turning red and Lily patted his back lightly.

"Stop, Logan. Just calm down."

"Asshole?" Charles eyes widened but before he could speak, Regina interrupted hurriedly.

"Mr. Anderson, we know that trying tobuy the baby from Lily was the wrong thing to do and we've apologized to her for it. We just want to be a part of our granddaughter's life. That's all. We're not going to – "

"Buy the baby?" Logan whispered. He turned back to look at Lily. "They tried to buy your baby?"

"Logan, listen to me. They – "

He shook his head and turned to glare at the elderly couple. "Get out of my house. Right now."

Regina gave Lily a frantic look. "Lily, please – "

"Get out of my house and don't ever contact Lily again." Logan's voice was low and dangerously quiet and Regina gave Charles a frightened look.

Charles took Regina's arm. "Let's go, Regina."

"Charles – "

"I said, let's go." Charles pulled her firmly from the living room and when Lily tried to follow them, Logan grabbed her arm.

"Let go of me, Logan." She hissed at him.

He blinked in surprise and dropped her arm. He followed her into the hallway and they watched in silence as Charles opened the door and pulled Regina outside.

"Lily, please call us. Please." Regina begged.

Before Lily could reply, Logan stepped around her and shut the door in their faces. Breathing heavily, he stared at Lily. She was glaring at him and, without speaking, she turned and stomped back into the living room.

He was two steps behind her and as she gathered up Regina's half-full tea cup he glared at her. "Why didn't you tell me they tried to buy the baby?"

She slid past him and stalked into the kitchen. He followed her and leaned against the doorway, blocking her in the kitchen. "Lily? I asked you a question."

"I didn't tell you because I didn't think it mattered. I wasn't going to sell the baby to them no matter what happened."

"You still should have told me." He said angrily.

"Why?"

"Why? Because – because I..."

He trailed off and she arched her eyebrow at him.

"You had already given me a job and a place to live. Because of you, I didn't even have to consider giving up my baby. Besides, you didn't need to be dragged into my personal problems. You're my employer, for heaven's sake."

"What did they want?" He asked abruptly.

"They wanted to apologize for trying to buy the baby and see if I would be willing to let them be a part of her life."

"No." He said immediately. "I don't want them anywhere near her."

"It's not your decision to make, Logan." She said gently.

"Lily, are you crazy? You can't let them near her. Not after how their son treated you. And especially not after they tried to buy the baby! Have you forgotten that they wouldn't even let you live in your own damn house?"

"I haven't forgotten." She said quietly. "But they are her grandparents and I'm not sure that denying them or her the right to be a part of each other's life, is the correct thing to do."

"Lily!" He gave her a look of exasperation and stepped forward to cup her arms. "They don't deserve to be anywhere near her. I know people like them. They think they can buy whatever they want and they don't care who they trample or hurt to get it."

"Logan, I know you're just trying to help but I – "

"You're not to see them again, Lily. Do you understand?"

She froze and then carefully backed away from him. "Don't you dare try and tell me what to do, Logan Anderson."

He hesitated, his face flushing, and she crossed her arms protectively over her belly. "I spent years living under Barry's thumb and his rules, and I'll never allow another man to treat me that way. Do *you* understand that?"

Hurt flooded through him. "You think I'm like Barry?"

"That isn't what I said. Don't put words in my mouth." She said angrily. "I know you're nothing like Barry but it doesn't mean that I'm going to allow you to dictate how I live my life."

"I'm not trying to – "

"You are." She said firmly. "You just stood there and told me that I'm not allowed to see Barry's parents."

"I didn't mean it that way. I just – I don't want them near our baby. Not after everything they've done to you. How can you trust them?"

She was giving him a strange look and his face burned dully when she said, "Logan, she's not *our* baby. She's my baby, and you need to trust that I know what's best for her and would never allow anyone to hurt her."

He stared mutely at her as she sighed and rubbed at her forehead. "I – I think that we need to take a step back, Logan. What happened a few nights ago was lovely and I enjoyed it very much but we both know that this is a mistake. You're my employer and having a relationship of a sexual nature is probably not the wisest move either of us could make. In a year Hazel will be in school and I'll be out of a job and out of your life. It's best if we maintain a strictly professional relationship from now on. Do you agree?"

"Is that what you want?" He asked quietly.

She hesitated. "It's what's best."

"But is it what you want?" He persisted.

"Please, Logan. Don't make this harder or more complicated than it already is. We both know – "

"Daddy!" Hazel came flying into the kitchen and Logan plastered a smile on his face and picked up the little girl.

"Hi, baby bug. How was your nap?"

"Good. I'm hungry." She kissed him on the cheek and then grinned at Lily.

"Can I have pasta for dinner, Lily?"

Lily nodded. "Yes. Why don't you take your daddy into the living room and he'll colour with you while I cook dinner."

"Okay." Hazel smiled at Logan and he hugged her tightly and, without looking at Lily, left the kitchen.

Chapter 13

"Lily? Will you tell me what's wrong?" Janet asked gently.

Lily stared into her tea. "Do you mean other than the fact that I'm nearly a week overdue and I'm so uncomfortable and my belly is so big I can barely fit through doors now?"

Janet laughed. "Yes, other than that."

Lily sighed, opened her mouth to tell Janet everything was fine and found herself spilling out the entire story of Barry's parents and what had happened between her and Logan.

Ten minutes later, as she stared shamefully at the table, she felt Janet's hand grip hers. "Lily, it's alright."

She looked around the busy coffee shop. No one was paying any attention to them and she gave Janet a miserable look, hoping the tears weren't about to start flowing down her face. "I'm so stupid, Janet."

"No, you're not. I told you before, there isn't anything wrong with being attracted to Logan."

Lily laughed humorlessly. "No, nothing wrong with it at all. Except that he's my employer and if I lose this job I'll be homeless and penniless with a baby to support."

"Do you believe Barry's parents really do just want to be in the baby's life?" Janet asked suddenly.

Lily mulled it over. "Yes. I've never seen Regina like that and even Charles seemed much more…subdued than he normally is."

"Then I think allowing them to be in her life is the right thing to do." Janet replied.

"You do?"

"I do." Janet said firmly. "Of course, I'm a firm believer that children should have lots of family around to help guide them and love them so take my advice with a grain of salt."

"Logan doesn't want them anywhere near her."

Janet smiled. "Logan cares for you. It makes him protective of both you and the baby, and I understand why he doesn't want them near either of you."

Lily frowned. "Logan only cares for me because he has a white knight complex and he believes I need saving."

Janet shrugged. "I don't think that's true, Lily."

"It is." She insisted. "Why else would he be attracted to me?"

Janet frowned at her. "Because you're gorgeous and sweet and good to him. Not to mention excellent with Hazel. Hazel loves you, that's plain to see, and just from watching you with her I know you'll make an excellent mother."

Lily blushed a little. "Thanks, Janet. I love Hazel too."

"I know you do, honey." Janet smiled at her. "Logan does care for you, and I believe it's more than just a stupid white knight complex, but you're right in that it doesn't mean he can tell you what to do with the baby. You have to make that decision for yourself, and if you want Barry's parents to be a part of her life then they should be. Don't let Logan's personal feelings cloud your judgment."

"I won't." Lily said firmly.

Janet took a sip of her coffee. "Now, how do you feel about Logan?"

"I – what?"

Janet grinned. "How do you feel about Logan? Do you love him?"

"I – I don't know. I care about him and I –" she stopped as she felt the familiar heat in her face and cheeks, "I want him desperately. It's all I can think about, which is ridiculous because I told him that I wanted it to be a strictly working relationship and for the last month he's done just that."

She sighed deeply before sipping at her tea. Janet was giving her a sympathetic look and Lily swallowed heavily. "Every night I lay in my bed and think about going to Logan's room. What kind of person does that make me? I tell him one thing yet inside I'm wishing desperately I'd never asked him to stay away from me."

Janet smiled at her. "People change their minds all the time, Lily. I'm sure if you went to Logan and – "

Lily shook her head. "It's been a month and he hasn't touched or looked at me like he has any interest. He's – he's not attracted to me anymore. I can't blame him. I look like I swallowed a beach ball."

Janet laughed so hard that the people at the table next to theirs glanced over. Lily flushed. "It's true."

Janet shook her head. "Logan is still attracted to you, trust me. The other night when you guys were over for dinner, he couldn't keep his eyes off of you. And I lost track of how many times he stopped himself from touching you."

Lily frowned. "I didn't notice."

"Of course you didn't. You're about to give birth, you're tired and sore, and Logan makes damn sure you're not looking when he's watching you."

Lily rubbed at her swollen belly. "What I need to do is stop thinking about sex with Logan and start thinking about getting this kid out of me. The doctor said she wanted to wait at least three more days after I was a week overdue before she'd consider inducing me. That's almost five more days. I'm not sure I can go five more days."

Janet grinned brightly at her. "I have the perfect solution."

Lily gave her a suspicious look. "Oh yeah? What's that?"

"Sex with Logan."

Lily, taking a sip of tea, coughed and sputtered. Janet leaned over and thumped her firmly on the back.

"Okay?"

"Yeah." Lily coughed again. "Although I'd like to know how sex with Logan is going to result in this baby making her grand entrance."

Janet laughed. "Seriously? You've never heard that having sex can bring on labour when you're close to your due date?"

Lily shook her head. "No. Are you just making this up because you know how much I want to sleep with Logan?"

"No, I swear I'm not." Janet snickered. "I was three days overdue with Nicole and the night before I went into labour, Rob and I had sex like three times. The very next morning – bam, I was in labour and Nicole was born not two hours later."

"Seriously?" Lily said doubtfully.

"Hand to God." Janet said solemnly. "Some women say that walking up and down stairs can help, but why do that when you can be having orgasms left and right? Seems like a no-brainer to me. I told you that pregnancy sex is the best sex ever right?"

"You did." Lily couldn't help but laugh.

"You had an orgasm with Logan. Was it super awesome, or what?" Janet asked cheerfully.

Lily turned bright red and Janet laughed and squeezed her arm. "I'm sorry, honey. I sometimes forget that not everyone is as open about their sex life as I am about mine."

* * *

Logan stepped out of the shower and towelled himself dry before pulling on a pair of shorts. He wandered into his bedroom and stared out the window into the darkness. He was feeling restless and grumpy and he was almost relieved to be going to work tomorrow. The last four days with Lily had been hell.

It felt like every day it got harder and harder to keep his hands to himself. He wanted Lily desperately and even though she had made it perfectly clear that she wanted just a working relationship, he wasn't sure how much longer he could live in the same house without touching her, kissing her, and making her his.

He sighed and shut the bedside lamp off, plunging the room into darkness. He pulled the quilt and the sheet back and then paused, cocking his head curiously. He could hear a faint rhythmic thumping noise and, every thirty seconds or so, the tell-tale squeak of the fourth stair. He waited for a few more moments and when it continued, crossed the bedroom and stepped curiously into the hallway.

He grunted softly in surprise. Lily, her head down and her dark hair hanging in her face, was climbing determinedly up and down the stairs. He watched as she disappeared down the staircase in to the darkness and then, a few seconds later, reappeared. She was wearing a thin tank top and her pale pink shorts and he stared at her breasts and her slender legs before clearing his throat.

"Lily? It's late. What are you doing?"

She didn't look up. "Climbing stairs."

"Why?"

She sighed. "Because Janet mentioned that climbing stairs repeatedly could bring on labour."

"I don't think it's good for your leg, Lily."

She didn't reply and before she could turn and stomp back down the stairs, he grabbed her arm lightly. "Stop, sweetheart. You're going to hurt your leg."

She finally looked at him. "I need this baby out, Logan. Do you hear me? I can't…"

She trailed off as she looked him up and down. He felt a small thrill go through him when her gaze met his and he could clearly see lust in her eyes. He had decided in the last month that she was no longer attracted to him, and to see her need for him now had him ready to carry her off to his bed. He took a deep breath as she joined him at the top of the staircase and stared at his naked chest.

"Why are you half-naked?" She asked almost angrily.

"I just got out of the shower." He wanted to touch her but he kept his hands clenched at his sides.

She reached out with a trembling hand and rubbed her fingers across his chest. He caught his breath, his cock hardening immediately in his shorts, and moaned lightly.

"I'm sorry." She whispered.

"Sorry for what?" He grunted.

"For touching you." She continued to stroke her fingers across his chest. "I told you we could only have a working relationship and here I am, touching you."

"I don't mind." He said hoarsely.

She gave him a searching look. "Do you still want me, Logan?"

"Yes."

She sighed. "I still want you too."

She dropped her hand and disappointment flooded through him. She stared at the floor and then said something so unexpected, he could only stare at her.

"Janet says that having sex can bring on labour."

When he didn't say anything, she sighed again. "It's probably not true, anyway. Good night, Logan."

She started to walk away and he caught her arm. "Lily, wait."

She turned to look at him. Her face was flushed and he could see the hard outline of her nipples against her shirt. His cock swelled in response and he took a deep breath.

"I know you said this should be a working relationship only and I – I agree. But if you wanted to um, try and induce labour, I'd be more than happy to help you with that."

She bit her bottom lip and he hurried on. "It can be just a one-time thing, Lily. I won't expect anything from you after tonight."

He wondered if his desperation was as apparent to her as it was to him. He was so anxious to have her in his bed, to feel her warmth sliding down over him, that he would take whatever she was willing to give him. Even if it was only one night and only because she was desperate to go into labour.

"I don't want to just use you, Logan." She whispered.

"I don't mind." He repeated. "I want to help you, Lily. Let me."

She hesitated and then reached out and touched his chest again. "I want you so badly, Logan."

His heart thumping in his chest, he put his arm around her waist and drew her up against him. "I want you too, Lily." He bent his head and kissed her throat. She moaned, her fingers digging into his chest and then turned her face towards him. He kissed her lightly, almost hesitantly, and then groaned loudly when she immediately pushed her tongue into his mouth. He sucked on it and she pressed herself against him as he reached around her and squeezed her ass.

"Just this one time. Okay, Logan?" She whispered when he released her mouth.

"Okay." Afraid she would change her mind, he bent and scooped her up and she gave a soft squeak of surprise.

He grinned at her and carried her into his bedroom, shutting the door behind them with his foot before crossing the room and setting her down gently next to the bed. He kissed her again, threading his fingers through her hair to hold her head firmly as he forced her mouth open wide so he could explore its warmth. She returned his kisses eagerly, her hands running over his back as he grabbed the hem of her tank top.

She lifted her arms and he pulled it over her head and dropped it to the floor before cupping one breast. He ran his thumb over her hard nipple and then bent his head, sucking it into his mouth and tracing it lightly with the tip of his tongue.

She gasped with pleasure, her hands moving restlessly through his hair as he sucked and licked, switching from one nipple to the other until she was moaning breathlessly and making soft pleading noises under her breath.

He slid his hands down over her hips and eased her panties down her legs. She stepped out of them and reached for the waistband of his shorts. He helped her take them off and she stared with delight at his erection. She reached out and took him into her hand, rubbing her thumb over the tip. He groaned loudly and thrust his hips against her.

She smiled up at him and he returned her smile, dipping his head to kiss her again. "You're so beautiful, Lily." He murmured.

"Thank you." She whispered shyly. "You're beautiful too."

He rubbed her bare belly before sliding his hand between her legs. At the feel of his fingers rubbing against her curls, she spread her legs and tightened her grip on his arms. "Please, Logan."

He rubbed her clit lightly and she made another whimper of need and pressed herself against him. "Make me come, Logan."

She blushed at her own boldness but he just smiled at her and dipped his head again to lick and nibble the line of her collarbone. "Whatever you want, sweetheart."

His fingers returned to her clit and rubbed firmly. She moaned loudly and clutched at him as he pressed and circled the swollen button. It took only a few minutes before she was stiffening in his arms, her hands digging into his flesh as her orgasm rushed through her. She collapsed against him, breathing harshly and her entire body trembling wildly.

"I love watching you come, Lily." He whispered into her ear.

"I want you inside of me." She murmured.

His cock throbbed at her words and without speaking he pressed her gently down onto the bed. He pulled a condom from the bedside drawer and ripped the packaging open, hurriedly rolling it on to his cock before leaning over her. She spread her legs eagerly and he knelt between them. His flat abdomen pressed into her belly as his cock grazed over her wetness and she shifted slightly. She groaned with frustration and he smiled at her.

"Maybe you should be on top."

"Yes." She muttered. She sat up and pushed him rather roughly to his back before climbing into his lap and straddling him. She was flushed and panting heavily, and she muttered a curse under her breath as she rubbed herself eagerly against him.

"Logan, I can't. It's not working." She wanted to cry with frustration. Her body was screaming for Logan's cock but with her belly in the way she couldn't find the correct angle.

"Shh." He soothed. He cupped her breasts and pulled lightly on her nipples. "We have all night, Lily."

"I can't wait." She gave him a look that was bordering on pouting and his grin widened.

He slid his hand under her belly and brushed it along her pussy. She moaned and thrust her hips at him. Even with her orgasm, her lower body was on fire with need and she thought she might go crazy if Logan didn't fuck her soon.

"Logan!" She cried out in desperation and he made another soothing noise before gripping his cock.

She rose up a little and moaned with pleasure when Logan guided his cock into her wet and waiting pussy. She pushed down on him, her walls stretching around his thick length and he made his own cry of pleasure.

"Fuck, Lily. You feel so damn good." He groaned.

She barely heard him. She had already started to ride him hard, her breasts jiggling with every bounce and her head thrown back and her eyes closed tightly. Logan's cock felt amazing. He was thick and hard and she felt so full, she could have cried with relief. She bounced faster, her breath coming in harsh pants, as his hands gripped her hips and helped lift her up and down.

"Oh, oh, oh!" She cried breathlessly. Warmth was growing in her belly, little lightning bolts of pleasure zipping up and down her thighs and with an almost animalistic cry, she thrust herself down hard upon him. His hands moved to cup her breasts and when his fingers pulled roughly on her rock-hard nipples, she threw her hand over her mouth to muffle her cry as she came wildly all over him.

His cock and thighs were soaked with her moisture and he thrust lightly in and out of her as she panted and shook above him. After a few minutes she opened her eyes and stared down at him. He smiled at her and she ran her thumb over his flat nipple, making him shudder, before planting her hands against his chest.

"Don't come yet." She abruptly demanded.

He couldn't stop the wide grin from crossing his face. He had never seen Lily like this, bossy and a little demanding, and he definitely liked it.

"Yes, ma'am." He winked at her and she flushed a little but began to ride him again. He took a few deep breaths and willed himself not to come as Lily's hot, tight pussy slid up and down his cock. His body was screaming for relief but he controlled his own need fiercely as Lily grabbed his hands and placed them on her breasts. He played with them – kneading and stroking and tugging on her nipples as she braced her hands against his broad chest and rode him at a frantic pace.

She suddenly squeezed him with her inner muscles and he made a loud groan, his hands tightening around her breasts. "Jesus, sweetheart. You're going to make me come."

"Yes." She panted. "I want you to come."

He blinked at her sudden change of mind but immediately began to thrust into her. She moaned and pushed down on to him eagerly. She was hanging on to him, her legs digging into his hips and her fingers curled around his shoulders and he wiggled his hand beneath her belly and stroked her pussy lightly. He rubbed at her clit, his cock throbbing and his balls tightening, and she made another low cry and her back arched. Wetness and warmth flooded his cock and her pussy tightened exquisitely around him.

He gasped her name and came inside of her with one last deep, pulsing thrust. His body shook beneath hers and her pussy milked his cock eagerly, pulling every ounce of his orgasm from him as she rocked against him.

They stayed locked together until his cock began to soften within her and only then did she climb off of him and collapse against the bed. He disposed of the condom and then slid in beside her, wrapping his arm around her and stroking her belly.

"Lily?" He said anxiously. "Did I hurt you? Are you okay?"

"You didn't hurt me." She sighed contently before yawning hugely. "I feel *so* much better, Logan. Your penis is awesome."

He laughed and she flushed a little but didn't open her eyes. "It is."

"Thank you, sweetheart." He kissed the tip of her nose and a small smile crossed her face before she frowned.

Without opening her eyes, she said, "Should I – do you want me to go back to my own room now?"

"No." He said immediately, his arm tightening around her. "Stay here with me tonight, Lily."

"I'd like that." She whispered.

"I'd like that too." He whispered back. He leaned over her and placed a gentle kiss on her mouth before resting his head on the pillow next to hers. She wiggled closer, pushing her naked ass against his crotch, and he was surprised to feel desire threading through him. His cock stirred against her ass and she rubbed against him in response.

Hesitantly, he reached up and cupped her breast. Her nipple was hard and tight and he plucked roughly at it, making her moan.

He made himself stop. "Lily, you should probably get some sleep. It's late and – "

She turned over awkwardly, her belly pushing against him, and stared up at him. "I'm not sleepy."

"You look sleepy."

"I'm not." She insisted. She reached down and stroked his cock with her small, soft hand. A sexy little grin crossed her face when she felt him start to harden. "I'm ready for round two, Logan."

"Whatever you want, sweetheart. Whatever you want." He grinned.

Chapter 14

"Logan? Hello – earth to Logan?"

Logan looked up at Rob. "What?"

"What do you mean – what?" Rob said irritably. "You've been spaced out all day, man. What the hell are you thinking about?"

"Nothing." Logan finished wiping down the counter in the kitchen as Rob leaned against the oven.

It was a lie. It had been a quiet day at the station, not a single call had come in, and he had spent most of it remembering how it had felt to be inside of Lily. He had just, in fact, been remembering the way Lily had looked on her hands and knees in his bed, her soft voice crying his name and begging him to fuck her.

He swallowed hard and turned away from Rob to hide his growing erection. Lily had been insatiable last night. Hell, they'd both been like horny teenagers and he had even impressed himself with his recovery time. He'd never had sex five times in one night, not even when he *was* a horny teenager, and he was a little surprised that he was still capable of getting an erection this morning. He had left Lily sleeping in his bed and he had kissed her softly before leaving for work. They had slept maybe a grand total of two hours last night and he should have been tired but he wasn't. In fact, he wondered if he would be able to convince Lily to sleep with him again tonight. She had said it was only a one-time thing but she was also anxious to go into labour. Maybe he could use that to his advantage, convince her to –

He snorted angrily to himself. He was being a selfish asshole and he'd be damned if he used Lily's desire to start labour to satisfy his own need. If she came to him tonight of her own accord he wouldn't turn her away, but he wouldn't make her feel like she had to keep sleeping with him. He wasn't –

"Hi Hazel!" Rob said cheerily.

Logan spun around to see Hazel and Lily standing in the doorway of the common area. He grinned and Lily flushed a little as Hazel ran to him.

"Hi daddy!"

"Hey, baby bug. I'm so glad to see you!" He picked her up and tossed her into the air before catching her and kissing her loudly on the cheek.

She giggled and kissed him on the mouth. "Are you having a good day?"

"I am. How about you?" He asked.

"Yep. Lily and I went to the park. A boy there pushed me and I fell down and hurt my knee but Lily kissed it better."

"That was nice of her." He glanced at Lily, wondering if he could convince her to kiss something on *his* body and, as if she'd read his mind, she flushed again.

He frowned. Lily looked tired and she had dark circles under her eyes. Guilt flooded through him and he hurried over to her.

"Lily, are you okay?" He asked anxiously.

She smiled at him. "Yes. Just a little tired, maybe."

He glanced behind him as he shifted Hazel in his arms. "I'm sorry." He said in a low voice. "I shouldn't have – "

She shook her head, interrupting him. "Don't apologize. I was the one who was um," she took a quick look at Hazel, "demanding, last night."

He grinned at her. "I didn't mind."

She gave him a searching look. "Are you sure?"

"Absolutely. I really like the demanding version of Lily."

She gave him a shy smile and he stroked her upper arm lightly. "Really liked it."

"I – I liked it too." She whispered.

"Liked what?" Hazel suddenly asked.

Lily gave him a wide-eyed look of panic and he quickly tickled Hazel. "Why did that boy push you, Hazel?"

She shrugged. "He was mean."

She suddenly giggled. "Guess what, daddy?"

"What's that, baby bug?"

"I found Lily sleeping in your bed this morning!" The little girl crowed loudly.

Logan winced and looked behind him. Rob was leaning against the counter, grinning broadly at him, and he gave the man a warning look before turning back to Lily. She was, not surprisingly, bright red and he gave her an apologetic look as Hazel patted his face with her small hand.

"I asked her if she was in your bed because she had a nightmare and she said yes. Did you make her feel better after her nightmare, daddy?"

Now Logan could feel his own face reddening and he gave Rob another pointed look when the man made a muffled choke of laughter. "Um, yeah, baby bug. I did."

"You're nice." Hazel said sweetly. "Can I have a drink of water?"

"Yes, you may." He carried Hazel toward the kitchen, not noticing when Lily flinched and placed her hand on her belly.

"Come see your Uncle Rob, baby girl." Rob said as Logan passed by him. He held out his arms and Hazel nodded agreeably. Logan transferred the little girl to Rob and took down a glass from the cupboard above the sink. He filled it halfway with water and gave it to Hazel.

"What do you say, Hazel?"

"Thank you, daddy." The little girl's voice was muffled as she lifted the glass to her mouth.

He squeezed Hazel's leg and then frowned when he heard Lily gasp behind him. He turned and took a few steps towards her. "Lily? What's wrong?"

She gave him a strange, frightened look. "I – I think my water just broke." Her gaze dropped downwards and they both stared at the spreading wetness darkening the front of her pants.

* * *

Logan stared wide-eyed at her and then hurried forward.

"Don't panic, don't panic." He said abruptly.

"I'm not panicking." Lily replied. "But I think – "

"Everything's cool." He interrupted her. "Both Rob and I have delivered babies before. Come over and lie on the couch and we'll – "

"Logan, I'm not having the baby right here." Lily protested. "I need to go to the hospital."

Still ignoring her, he grabbed her arm and tried to tug her to the couch. "Women have babies every day, Lily. The important thing is that you don't panic. Take some deep breaths and – "

"Logan – "

"Everything is going to be just fine." Despite his assurances he could feel the panic building inside of him and he tamped it down grimly. Lily would be fine. He just needed to remember his training and –

"Logan!" Rob's deep voice shook him out of his growing panic and he stared at the other man, his breath rushing in and out of him.

"You need to stop panicking." Rob said with a hint of laughter in his voice. "Calm down, man. You're a firefighter for God's sake. You deal with stuff like this all the time."

"I'm not panicking!" Logan said, his voice shrill with panic.

Rob actually did laugh this time as Lily put her hand on his arm. "Logan, look at me. I'm fine but I should go to the hospital. Can I leave Hazel here with you, or should I call Janet and ask her to come and get her?"

He stared blankly at her for a moment. "What do you mean?"

"Can you get someone else to cover your shift so you can look after Hazel while I'm in the hospital or should I call Janet?" She said patiently.

"You're not going to the hospital by yourself!" He shouted.

Hazel, her eyes wide and frightened, gave a small cry. "Daddy! What's wrong with Lily? Is it the baby? Is it hurting mommy?"

Logan made himself take a deep breath before turning to Hazel still nestled in Rob's arms. "No, baby bug. Lily's okay. But the baby is ready to be born and daddy has to take her to the hospital. You're going to stay with Uncle Rob and Aunt Janet while we're at the hospital."

"No!" Hazel shouted. "I want to go with you and mommy!"

"You can't, honey." Lily said soothingly. "But as soon as the baby is born, you can come to the hospital and see her, okay?"

Hazel shook her head and began to sob. "No. I want to stay with you."

Logan plucked her from Rob's arms and hugged her. "You have to be a big girl right now, Hazel, and be brave. You'll have fun at Uncle Rob's and before you know it, the baby will be here and you can see her."

Hazel sniffed loudly. "I really want to stay with mommy. Please, daddy."

"You can see mommy after the baby is born." Logan said distractedly. He was staring at his watch, wondering how long it had been since Lily's water had broken. "Are you having a contraction, Lily?"

She shook her head. "No, I feel fine. Just a bit crampy. You don't have to come to the hospital with me, Logan. I can – "

She suddenly stiffened, a look of pain crossing her face, and hunched over a little before grabbing her belly. Logan handed Hazel to Rob and hurried over. He placed his hand on her belly and checked his watch.

"Take some deep breaths, sweetheart." He said anxiously. "Nice and deep."

Lily took a deep breath before blowing it out in a harsh rush. Her body relaxed and she straightened. "Better."

"Good." He glanced at Rob. "I'm going to drive Lily to the hospital. Can you take Hazel?"

"Yes, no problem." Rob said immediately. "Hold out your hand, Logan."

"What?" Logan said impatiently.

"Hold out your hand, man."

Rolling his eyes, Logan held out his hand and Rob stared at his badly-shaking hand with another hint of amusement. "You're in no condition to drive."

"I can drive." Lily said helpfully.

Logan stared at her. "Are you crazy? You're in labour! There's no way in hell you're driving"

"Logan, I'm not – "

"No." He said firmly. "You're in no condition to drive."

"Either are you." Rob laughed. "C'mon, we'll take the truck." He tickled Hazel. "Do you want to go for a ride in the fire truck, honey?"

Hazel nodded eagerly, her tears forgotten, and Rob grinned at her. "Good. Let's get your mommy to the hospital so she can have her baby, shall we?"

* * *

The short and plump doctor entered the room, pulling a white jacket over her yoga pants and tank top. "I hear you're ready to have your baby, Lily."

"Yeah." Lily panted.

"Excellent!" The doctor beamed at her and placed one hand on her belly. "How are you feeling?"

"Tired." Lily replied. "I'm sorry to bring you in on your day off, Dr. Stevenson."

"Oh I don't mind." The doctor said cheerfully. "I was just doing some outdoor yoga at the park."

Logan, standing next to the bed and holding Lily's hand, gave her an impatient look. "She's been in labour for six hours and the contractions are two minutes apart."

The doctor gave him a curious look. "And you are?"

"Logan Anderson."

"He's a friend." Lily said. "He's a firefighter so he has some experience with – "

She made a sudden moan and gripped Logan's hand tightly. "Logan." She whimpered.

"Okay sweetheart okay." He bent over her and stroked her arm. "Breathe through it."

After a few minutes, Lily's body relaxed and she collapsed against the bed, moaning softly.

"Good job, Lily." Dr. Stevenson smiled at her. "Let's see how far you're dilated."

As she went to the end of the bed, Lily stared up at Logan. "It hurts so much, Logan."

"I know, sweetheart." He said helplessly.

"I'm really starting to regret the decision to not do an epidural." She said through gritted teeth.

As Dr. Stevenson popped back up, she gave the doctor a frantic look. "Is it too late for an epidural?"

"I'm afraid so, Lily." Dr. Stevenson smiled at her. "It's time to start pushing."

* * *

Lily, groaning loudly, collapsed against Logan. It was an hour later and she had been pushing off and on for the entire time. She was sweaty and exhausted, and Logan smoothed her hair back from her forehead. He was tucked behind her in the bed and she leaned against his chest, moaning softly, as Dr. Stevenson gave the nurse next to her a look that made Logan's blood freeze in his veins.

"Lily? I need you to push again. Alright?" The doctor said softly.

"I can't." Lily groaned. "I'm so tired."

"I know, but I need you to give me one more big push. C'mon, Lily. One more push."

"Logan…" Lily whimpered.

"You can do it, sweetheart. Just one more push." He whispered.

She stared at him and then nodded. "Okay." She whispered back.

"Push, Lily. Push now." The doctor said loudly.

Groaning, fresh sweat breaking out on her forehead and her hands squeezing his until they went numb, Lily pushed as hard as she could. A scream of pain tore from her throat and Logan's stomach rolled with nausea.

"Stop pushing, Lily!" The doctor suddenly shouted and Lily collapsed against him again, panting heavily as the doctor looked at the screen that monitored the baby's heartbeat.

She had a worried look on her face and as she stood and approached Lily, Logan could feel his heart thudding wildly in his chest.

"Lily, look at me."

Lily turned her gaze wearily to the doctor. "What?"

"The baby's not moving down the birth canal the way she should. Her heartbeat is way higher than it should be and I'm afraid she's in distress. I'm worried that the cord might be wrapped around her neck. I think we need to do a C-section."

"What?" Lily gave her a look of panic and Dr. Stevenson squeezed her shoulder soothingly.

"I think it's best for both you and the baby if we do an emergency caesarean."

"Are you sure?" Lily whispered.

"Yes, I am." The doctor replied firmly.

Lily stared up at Logan. Her gaze was wide and frightened and he bent his head and kissed her softly on the mouth. "It'll be okay, sweetheart."

She nodded and turned back to the doctor. "Okay."

"Good." The doctor turned to the nurse. "Let's get her prepped for surgery."

She eyed Logan. "Mr. Anderson, you can wait in the waiting room and we'll let you know – "

"No!" Lily shouted immediately. "I want him in there with me."

She squeezed Logan's hand and gave him a look of panic. "Don't leave me, Logan."

"I'm not going anywhere, sweetheart." He said quickly. "I promise."

She nodded with relief and squeezed his hand as Logan gave her a look of confidence that he didn't feel. "Everything will be fine. You'll be holding your baby girl before you know it."

* * *

"Logan?"

Logan looked up from the vending machine when he heard Janet's voice. She was hurrying towards him. Rob, carrying Hazel in his arms, was right behind her and Logan smiled at them both.

"How is she?"

"She's good. Both her and the baby are fine." He took Hazel from Rob and kissed her soft cheek.

"Hi, baby bug."

"Hi, daddy." Hazel whispered. "Is Lily okay?"

"Yes. She had to have surgery to have the baby, but both her and the baby are doing just fine." He picked up the cup of coffee from the vending machine and sipped at it, making a face at its thick, bitter taste.

"Can I see her?"

"Yes, but just for a few minutes. Lily's very tired and she needs her rest."

"Okay."

He handed Hazel to Janet. "She's in room 303. Tell her I'll be up in a minute, okay?"

"Sure." Janet squeezed Hazel. "C'mon, baby bug. Let's go see Lily and the baby."

She carried Hazel down the hall as Logan sat down in one of the hard plastic chairs in the lobby. He set the coffee down on the side table and buried his face in his hands.

"You okay, man?" Rob had sat down beside him and he rested his hand on Logan's shoulder.

Logan nodded. "Yeah, I'm good."

"Are you sure?"

He nodded again. "Yeah. The surgery went really well and Lily's okay."

"So, what's wrong?"

He shook his head and then glanced up at Rob. "Lily asked me to stay with her and I said of course. I was there when they pulled the baby out and…"

He sighed deeply and looked at his trembling hands. "Erin wouldn't even let me in the room when she had Hazel. Do you remember?"

"I remember." Rob said quietly.

"I was Hazel's father and I didn't get to see her being born or cut the cord because Erin was a selfish, cold bitch."

"She was." Rob agreed.

"Lily not only wanted me in there with her but when the surgeon thought I was the baby's father and asked if I wanted to cut the cord, Lily let me."

Logan swallowed thickly and stared at Rob. "She's so beautiful, Rob. She looks just like Lily. She has thick, dark hair and a perfect round head and when Lily was holding her, the baby opened her eyes and she – she looked at me."

Rob squeezed his shoulder and Logan shook his head in wonderment. "I fell in love with her right then and there."

Rob didn't say anything and Logan gave him a quick look. "The baby, I mean."

"Yeah, I know you meant the baby." Rob replied. He paused and then clapped Logan on the back. "It's certainly not Lily you're talking about. You've been in love with her for the last three months."

Logan opened his mouth to protest and Rob laughed loudly when nothing came out. "C'mon, man. Your woman's waiting for you."

Chapter 15

"Rachel is a beautiful name." Janet smiled at her before staring down at the tiny baby in her arms. "A beautiful name for a beautiful baby."

"Thank you." Lily said softly as she cuddled Hazel on the hospital bed.

"How much did she weigh?"

"Seven pounds, two ounces."

"That's a good weight. Congratulations, honey."

"Thanks, Janet." Lily kissed the top of Hazel's head.

"How are you feeling?"

"A little sore but not too bad."

"Good. Any idea how long you have to stay in the hospital?"

Lily shrugged. "No more than a couple of days, I hope."

"I want you to come home tonight." Hazel suddenly said.

"I can't, honey. I have to stay a little longer and then I'll be home."

The little girl started to pout and Lily hugged her closer. "It won't be too long, honey."

Rob and Logan entered the room and Rob bent over the baby in Janet's arms. He brushed his fingers across her cheek before turning to Lily. "Congrats, Lily. She's gorgeous, just like her mama."

"Thanks, Rob." Lily smiled at him as Logan took her hand and squeezed it briefly before ruffling Hazel's hair.

"Do you want to hold the baby, Hazel?" Lily asked.

The little girl nodded and Logan eagerly eased the sleeping baby out of Janet's arms and cradled her close to his chest. He kissed the top of her soft head.

"Sit up straight, baby bug." He instructed.

Hazel sat up in the bed and straightened her legs. Logan carefully transferred the baby to her lap as Lily put her arm around Hazel and helped support her head. Logan squeezed in next to Lily and the three of them stared down at the baby.

"She's wrinkly." Hazel announced.

Lily laughed. "Yes, she's a little bit wrinkled. She'll fill out."

Hazel continued to study her for a moment. "She's okay, I guess."

"Hazel." Logan chided gently as Lily laughed again.

Hazel glanced up at Lily. "Do you love her more than me?"

Lily shook her head. "No, honey. I love you both equally."

"Okay." Satisfied, Hazel looked down at the baby again.

There was the quiet click of a camera and Logan and Lily looked up to see Janet with her camera in her hand.

"Sorry." She grinned at them. "I can't help it."

Lily smiled at her as Hazel continued to look at the baby. "Hi, baby."

"Her name is Rachel, baby bug." Logan said.

"Hi Rachel." Hazel bent and kissed the baby's head before looking at Logan. "Can we go home now, daddy?"

"You're going to stay at Aunt Janet and Uncle Rob's house tonight, baby bug. I'm going to stay at the hospital with Lily."

Hazel's face crumpled. "I don't want to stay there. I want to stay with you, daddy."

"Hazel – "

"That's fine, honey." Lily interrupted Logan. "Daddy will go home with you tonight."

Logan frowned at her and she gave him a quick shake of her head.

Janet stood up and held out her hand. "Hazel, why don't you come with Uncle Rob and I back to the car. We'll grab your jacket and your dad can meet us down there after he says goodbye to Lily."

"Sure!" Hazel said happily.

Logan lifted Rachel out of Hazel's arms and held her as Hazel hugged and kissed Lily. "Bye, Lily. I'll see you later, alligator."

"In a while, crocodile." Lily smiled at her and patted her bottom as she squirmed off the bed and took Janet's hand.

"Congratulations again, Lily. I'll pop by tomorrow, okay?" Janet said.

"Yes. Thank you, Janet." Lily reached out and squeezed the woman's hand and Rob gave her a brief wave before they left with Hazel.

Logan was still sitting beside her and he was staring at the baby in his arms with wonderment. "Hello, Rachel." He whispered. "I'm so glad you're here."

Lily blinked back the tears as Logan kissed Rachel's forehead before glancing at her.

"Lily, I think I should stay with you and Rachel tonight. You've had surgery and you might need my help in the night."

She smiled at him. "I think it's better for Hazel if you go home with her. She's already worried and a little jealous. Let's not make that worse, okay?"

"Yeah, you're right." He sighed. "I'll take her out for supper and maybe ice cream. She'd like that."

"She would." Lily smiled again at him. "Logan, thank you."

"For what?" He gave her a surprised look.

"For everything. For staying with me, for giving me a place to live and a job. I appreciate it so much."

"Of course." He hesitated and then leaned in and kissed her lightly on the mouth. "If you need anything, just call my cell. It doesn't matter what time it is."

"I will." Lily promised. "Now go home and get some sleep, okay?"

He nodded and kissed Rachel again before handing her back to Lily. "I'll see you tomorrow, baby bee."

A small grin crossed Lily's face. "Baby bee?"

He flushed. "Sorry."

"It's fine." She smiled at him and he couldn't resist leaning in and kissing her a final time.

"Promise you'll call me if you need me."

"I promise."

"Hazel and I will be back first thing in the morning."

"I know. I'll see you then."

He slid off the bed and hesitated. "Are you sure, Lily?"

She nodded. "Yes. I'll be fine and I'll call you if I need anything."

He took a deep breath. "Okay, see you in the morning."

"Good night, Logan."

* * *

Lily stared fixedly at the phone in her hand. She had just finished feeding Rachel and the nurse had taken the baby back to the nursery. She had hoped that Rachel could stay with her but because of the C-section and without anyone to stay with her, they wouldn't allow it. The nurse had promised to bring Rachel back for her next feeding and after kissing the baby's soft head, Lily had nodded and watched them take her away.

She sighed and quickly dialed the number before she could change her mind. Her fingers twisted nervously in her lap as the phone rang and she cleared her throat as Regina's familiar voice said hello.

"Hi Regina. It's Lily."

"Hi Lily." Regina said warmly. "How are you?"

"I'm good. I – I just wanted to let you know that I had the baby."

"You did? That's wonderful! How are you feeling?"

"Good. I had to have a C-section but both the baby and I are doing just fine."

"That's really great. Thank you for calling us."

"You're welcome."

Regina paused. "How much did she weigh?"

"Seven pounds, two ounces."

"That's a good weight."

"Yes. She's very healthy, she has all her fingers and all her toes and she has dark hair."

"Good." Regina said happily. "What did you name her?"

"Her name is Rachel. Rachel Annabelle."

There was silence on the other end of the phone and after a moment, Lily said, "Regina? Are you still there?"

There was loud sniffing and then Regina cleared her throat roughly. "Yes, I'm still here. Thank you, Lily. I can't tell you how much it means to me that you used the name Annabelle."

"You're welcome." Lily replied softly.

There was another hesitation and then Regina said, "Could we see her?"

Lily hesitated. "Yes, but can you give me a few days? I'm still in the hospital but once I'm home and settled I'll give you a call and you can drop by and visit. Okay?"

"Yes, of course." The relief in Regina's voice was undeniable. "Thank you so much, Lily."

"You're her grandparents. You deserve the right to meet her." Lily answered. "Listen, I should go. I'll call you in a few days, okay?"

"Of course. We'll talk to you soon, Lily."

"Bye, Regina."

Lily hung up the phone before lying back in the bed and staring up at the ceiling. Despite Logan's protests, she knew she was doing the right thing.

Chapter 16

"Daddy? What are you doing?" Hazel stuck her head into his office and stared at him curiously.

"Just thinking, baby bug."

He smiled at her as she stood on his feet and grabbed his hands. He walked her down the hallway and into Lily's room, staring thoughtfully at the crib crammed into the corner, the boxes of clothes and baby supplies piled at the foot of Lily's bed and the change table jammed under the window.

"Hazel?"

"What?" She was playing with some of the stuffed toys in the basket next to the crib.

"What do you think about giving Rachel her own room? Do you think Lily would like it if we turned my office into a nursery?"

Hazel shrugged. "I don't know."

"I bet she would like it. We could paint the room and decorate it before Lily and Rachel come home. We could make it a surprise for them."

"What colour?" Hazel asked as she left the toys and stood next to him.

"What colour do you think we should paint it?"

"Pink." She said quickly. "Pink is for girls."

"Then we'll paint it pink. Come on, I need to call your Uncle Rob."

"Why?"

"Because if we want to get this room done before Lily comes home, we're going to need some help."

* * *

Lily held Rachel closer and stared down at her sweet face. An overwhelming feeling of love swept through her and she could feel tears starting in her eyes. She'd had no clue how deeply she would fall in love with her from the moment she saw her and she was a little overwhelmed by it.

She shifted the baby in her arms and Rachel suckled harder at her nipple. The nurse popped her head around the curtain. "Still eating?"

"Yes." Lily smiled at her.

The nurse nodded. "She's a good eater and she's latched on very well. That's good."

Lily smiled again. "I'm pretty happy about that. I was worried about breastfeeding and how it would go."

"It seems to be going just fine. I'll leave you for a bit longer. Just ring the bell if you need anything, okay?"

"I will, thanks."

The nurse disappeared and Lily stared blankly at the curtain. Despite her happiness, despite the fact that her baby was healthy and she'd actually gotten a good night sleep, she couldn't stop the ball of worry in her stomach from growing.

She looked up when Janet slipped past the curtain and grinned at her. "Hello, gorgeous."

"Hi, Janet."

The redhead plopped down in the chair. "How's she doing?"

"Good. She's eating really well."

"Excellent. Did you get any sleep last night?"

"Quite a bit, actually. I couldn't keep her in my room because of the surgery so the nurses just brought her to me for feedings."

"Enjoy that while it lasts." Janet winked at her. "How do you feel?"

"Oh fine."

Janet cocked her head. "Are you sure?"

"Yes."

"Not weepy or worried or sad?"

Lily shrugged. "A little worried, maybe."

"About what?"

She sighed. "The hospital bill for starters. I don't have insurance and I can only imagine how much the bill will be. I have no idea how I'm going to pay it."

Janet gave her a sympathetic look as Lily blinked back the tears. "I told Logan when he hired me that I would come right back to work after the pregnancy. That there would be no problems. Dr. Stevenson told me I can't lift anything heavier than Rachel for six weeks, and I have to limit my bending and stretching. How am I supposed to look after Hazel?"

"Honey, I wouldn't worry – "

"And I told Logan that if he hired me I would take the baby and stay somewhere else for the four days that he wasn't working so the noise didn't bother them. I thought it would be simple enough to just stay in a motel, you know? But again, I wasn't expecting to have a C-section and I never even thought about the stupid hospital bill. There's no way in hell I'll have enough money for a motel."

Lily was starting to cry and Janet reached out and squeezed her hand before passing her a tissue.

"Thanks." Lily sniffed. She stared down at Rachel, still suckling hungrily at her breast, and stroked her dark hair.

"Honey, you don't have to worry about finding someplace else to live when Logan's at home. Logan isn't going to let you or your baby live in a motel four days a week. I guarantee it." Janet said quietly.

Lily shook her head. "If I can't even do my job, look after Hazel, why would he even keep me on?"

Janet squeezed her hand again. "Hazel is four and quite self-sufficient. She'll learn quickly that you can't pick her up and that she'll have to do some stuff for herself. It'll be an adjustment period but she'll get used to it. And I really don't think Logan will care if you're not cooking or cleaning for six weeks."

"That's my job." Lily whispered miserably. "If I'm not doing it, he won't −"

"He won't care." Janet interrupted firmly. "Just trust me on this."

"I don't want to take advantage of him." Lily gave her a timid look. "I don't want to be like Erin where I use his niceness against him. It's not fair of me − "

"Honey, you are nothing like Erin. Nothing. Don't ever compare yourself to her. Do you understand me?" Janet said sternly.

Lily nodded and wiped at her eyes with the tissue.

"Has Logan been here today?"

Lily nodded again. "Yes, he and Hazel were here as soon as visiting hours started. They stayed for a couple of hours but they have some top secret project they're working on. I have no idea what it is, but Hazel was really excited about it."

Janet grinned and said nothing as Lily stroked Rachel's soft hair again. "He said he would come back later today."

"I sure did." Logan said cheerfully as he slipped past the curtain. "Hi, Janet."

"Hi, Logan."

She watched as Logan bent and kissed Rachel's head. "She was eating when I left this morning." He grinned at Lily. "Has she even stopped?"

Lily laughed. "Yes."

Logan placed his finger in Rachel's hand and grinned like a little boy when her tiny fist closed around it. "Who's my good girl?"

The baby let go of Lily's nipple and made a short wail. Logan made a soothing noise before kissing her head again.

"Sorry, baby bee."

"She just needs to be burped." Lily lifted her to her shoulder and patted her back gently as Logan sat at the end of the bed and rubbed Lily's leg through the blanket.

"How are you feeling?"

"Good. Dr. Stevenson was in earlier and she thinks we can go home tomorrow afternoon."

"That's great!" Logan said delightedly.

"It really is." Lily sighed.

Logan studied her for a moment. "Have you been crying?"

She shook her head and handed Rachel to him. "No. Could you hold her for a minute? I need to use the bathroom."

"Yes." Logan took Rachel eagerly and held her against his shoulder. He patted her back as Lily eased out of the bed and disappeared into the bathroom.

Logan glanced at Janet. "Was she crying?"

Janet nodded. "Yes. She's worried because she told you that she could go right back to work after having the baby. The C-section has changed that, and she's afraid you're going to fire her because she can't look after Hazel properly."

Logan sighed. "That's ridiculous. Hazel's a big girl, and she understands that Lily won't be able to pick her up or do certain things with her for a little while."

"She's also scared that you're going to make her honour her promise to stay in a motel with Rachel when you're not working."

"What?" Logan gave her a look of disbelief. "There's no way in hell I'm letting Lily stay in a motel with Rachel."

"I know." Janet replied. "But Lily thinks you might. You know how she is. She's always so afraid she'll be fired, or that she'll do something wrong and upset you."

Logan sighed with frustration. "I don't know how to make her stop believing that."

Janet gave him a sympathetic look. "She's a smart girl. She'll figure it out eventually."

The bathroom door opened and Lily carefully walked back to the bed. She climbed in gingerly and smiled at Logan. "I can take her back if you're tired of holding her."

He shook his head. "No, I like holding my baby bee."

Her smile widened and he grinned at her as Janet stood and kissed Lily on the forehead. "I'm going to go, Lily. I'll come by later tonight, alright?"

"Alright. Thank you so much, Janet." Lily squeezed her hand as Janet kissed Rachel's soft head and then Logan's cheek before leaving the room.

"Was work okay with you taking today off?" She asked as Logan rubbed Rachel's back.

He nodded. "Yeah, it was no problem."

"Good, good." She gave him a nervous look. "Logan, I just want you to know that despite the C-section, I'll still take good care of Hazel. I already feel much better than yesterday and I think the six week thing is more of a suggestion than a rule. I can – "

"Lily, stop." He said gently. "The six weeks is not a suggestion, it's a requirement. You're not to be lifting anything heavier than Rachel, do you understand?"

She didn't reply and he could see tears starting in her eyes.

"Besides," he continued cheerfully, "I've taken the next two weeks off so I'll be around to help with Hazel and Rachel, as well as the cooking and housework, for the first little bit anyway."

She gaped at him. "You what?"

"I've taken two weeks off."

"But, but," she sputtered, "how?"

"I've got vacation and I talked with Bill this morning about taking it right now. He didn't have a problem with it and actually encouraged me to take some time off."

"Logan, I – that's so nice of you." Lily replied. She was beginning to weep and he reached out and brushed the tears away with his thumb.

"Don't cry, Lily. And, by the way, there's no way in hell I'm letting you and the baby bee stay in a motel so don't bother bringing it up. Alright?"

Her bottom lip trembling, she nodded. "Alright. Thank you, Logan."

"You're welcome, sweetheart."

A man, holding a massive, plush teddy bear, strolled into the room. "Lily Castro?" He asked in a bored voice.

"Yes?" Lily replied.

"Delivery for you." He propped the teddy bear up in the chair beside the bed and handed her an envelope.

"Thank you."

The man, he wore a shirt that had "Gifts by Barb" embroidered across the left breast, nodded and left as Lily opened the envelope.

She opened the card and read silently. Logan frowned when fresh tears began to drip down her cheeks.

"Lily? What's wrong?"

"Nothing." She murmured. She set the card aside and smiled at him.

"Who's the bear from?" He prompted.

"Regina and Charles."

"They know you had the baby?" He asked guardedly.

"Yes. I called Regina yesterday and let her know."

"Have they seen her yet?" Logan unconsciously held Rachel a little closer.

She shook her head and wiped the tears from her face.

"Why are you crying, Lily?"

She sighed. "They've paid my hospital bill."

"They what?"

"They paid the hospital bill."

"That's nice of them."

She gave him a dry look. "Just say what you want to say, Logan."

He shifted Rachel in his arms and stared at her sweet face for a moment. "I'm worried that they're trying to bribe you into seeing Rachel."

"They might be." She acknowledged.

"Are you going to let them see her?" He asked.

She sighed. "They're her grandparents, Logan."

"I know that, Lily, but they don't deserve to see her. They tried to buy her for God's sake." He said angrily.

"They know that was wrong, Logan. They just want the chance to be a part of her life." She said softly.

"I don't want them seeing her." He said stubbornly.

"I know. You've made that perfectly clear." She sighed.

"Lily, I – "

Rachel let out a lusty cry in his arms and he patted her bottom gently. "It's alright, baby bee."

"She probably needs to be changed." Lily held out her arms and Logan passed the baby to her. As she began to change Rachel's diaper, cooing softly to the tiny baby, he gave her a troubled look.

* * *

"It's so good to be home." Lily sighed.

Holding Hazel's hand she walked into the living room and shrugged out of her jacket. Logan, carrying Rachel in her car seat, winked at Hazel. The little girl was nearly vibrating with excitement and she tugged on Lily's hand.

"Lily, come upstairs with me."

"Sure, honey." Lily smiled at the little girl. "I should probably have a hot shower while Rachel is still sleeping."

"Do you need help up the stairs?" Logan asked as Lily limped up the stairs gingerly.

She shook her head. "No, I just need to go slowly."

When they reached the top of the stairs, Lily turned to head toward her room and frowned when Hazel tugged again on her hand. "Come this way, Lily."

"Honey, where are we going?" She looked over her shoulder at Logan who, swinging Rachel's car seat back and forth gently, just shrugged innocently.

Lily followed Hazel to Logan's office. Hazel, grinning happily, opened the door and ran into the room.

"Surprise!" She shouted.

Lily stared at the transformed room. "Oh my God." She whispered.

"Do you like it? I helped Daddy paint it and I said we should paint it pink because Rachel's a girl!" Hazel shouted again.

"Not so loud, baby bug." Logan said gently. "Rachel is sleeping, remember?"

"Sorry, daddy." Hazel pulled Lily into the room. "Do you like it, Lily?"

"I love it." Lily said immediately. "It's the most beautiful nursery I've ever seen."

She studied the room carefully. The walls were painted a soft pink and large yellow flower stickers had been placed on one wall in an artful display. There was a change table and a rocking chair and a small dresser that had a vase of flowers and a large photo frame display.

She walked to the dresser and stared at the framed pictures. Two of them were the maternity pictures Janet had taken of her and Hazel. The third one was the picture Janet had taken at the hospital of the four of them. She stared at the picture and blinked back the tears.

"Lily?" Logan was standing beside her and he put his arm around her waist. "Are you alright?"

"Yes." She whispered. She hugged him, wrapping her arms around his waist and clinging tightly to him. "Thank you, Logan. I love the nursery so much. I can't believe you gave up your office."

He shrugged. "Rachel deserves a nursery and it was too crowded in your room. Speaking of which – I thought maybe we should switch rooms. My room is closer to the nursery and – "

"No." Lily shook her head. "You're not giving up your bedroom. You've already done way too much for us."

"I don't mind. I – "

"No." She said firmly. "It's not that far away and for the first little while, Rachel will be in my room anyway."

"Daddy, can I sleep in the crib tonight?" Hazel asked.

Logan shook his head. "No, baby bug. You're a big girl and big girls sleep in their big girl beds, remember?"

"I guess." Hazel sighed. "Lily, will you read me a story?"

"Lily's going to have a shower, baby bug. She's tired and she needs to rest lots for the first little while." Logan replied.

Hazel, her lower lip quivering and her eyes filling with tears, sniffed miserably. "I want her to read to me."

Lily took Hazel's hand. "Come on, honey. Pick out a book from your room and we'll lie on my bed and I'll read it to you while daddy watches Rachel, okay?"

"Okay." Hazel skipped out of the room and Logan gave Lily an earnest look.

"Lily, you don't need to baby Hazel. I had a talk with her yesterday about how you would be busy with Rachel, and she needed to be patient and – "

"I don't mind." Lily interrupted. "She's uncertain and nervous about the new baby, and I think it's natural for her to need a little extra attention. Would you mind watching Rachel?"

He shook his head. "No, of course not."

She squeezed his hand before kissing his cheek. "Thank you, Logan. I love the nursery."

He stopped her before she could leave and kissed her on the mouth. "I'm glad you like it."

* * *

"Lily?" Logan opened his bedroom door and peered worriedly into the hallway at her. "Is Rachel okay?"

It was just after midnight and he had been lying awake in the dark, wishing he was in Lily's room with her, when he had heard Rachel crying.

She nodded and held the wailing baby closer. "Yes. She's just wet and hungry and stupid me left the diapers in the nursery. I'm sorry to wake you."

"That's alright." He frowned when Lily winced and placed a hand on her abdomen briefly.

He took Rachel from her. "Here, I'll change Rachel. Climb into my bed and I'll bring her to you when I'm done."

"I can go back to my room." She protested.

He shook his head. "My bed is more comfortable. Go on, sweetheart. I'll just be a minute."

He carried Rachel into the nursery before she could argue.

Lily climbed carefully into Logan's bed. He was right, she thought ruefully, his bed was more comfortable. She tucked the pillow behind her and smiled when she heard Logan singing softly to Rachel. After a few moments, he carried the still-crying baby into the room and placed her in Lily's arms. As Lily began to feed her, he left his bedroom and returned with the bassinet. Without speaking, he placed the bassinet on the floor beside the bed before climbing into the bed next to Lily.

He leaned over and kissed Rachel's soft head as she suckled noisily at Lily's breast. "Is my baby bee a hungry girl?" He whispered before kissing her again.

He sat back and rested his large hand on Lily's thigh. "She's a good eater."

Lily smiled. "She certainly is. Logan, I'm sorry. I didn't mean to wake you. I promise I'll be more organized tomorrow night."

He shook his head. "You didn't wake me. Besides, I don't mind. I used to help Erin with Hazel at night."

"Did you?" She asked quietly.

He nodded. "Erin didn't do well without much sleep and Hazel was a colicky baby." He didn't tell her that it had been a necessity. Erin had refused to do anything but feed Hazel during the night and Logan had spent many nights walking and soothing the fussy baby.

Lily touched his hand hesitantly. "Logan? I know I keep saying this but thank you. I'll never be able to repay you for everything you've done for me and I want you to know that I'm so grateful."

He leaned over and kissed her lightly on the mouth. "I'm happy to help, Lily. Besides, you deserve it."

He put his arm around her and she leaned against him. They watched Rachel eat and Logan stroked Lily's hair. He thought about what Rob had said in the hospital, about being in love with Lily, and he closed his eyes. Was he in love with Lily? He cared about her a great deal but he really did have a white knight complex, despite his protests. Was he helping her because of that or because of something deeper? He sighed lightly. He needed to be careful. Although Lily was nothing like Erin, he couldn't start another relationship based on his need to take care of someone. It had been an absolute nightmare with Erin and he wouldn't put Hazel through that again. Besides, his feelings for Lily didn't matter much. She had made it perfectly clear that what had happened between them was just a way to induce labour. She might have wanted him but she also wasn't interested in a relationship with her employer.

He needed to take a step back and give Lily her space. The distance would help him decide whether his feelings for her were based on his desire to help or something deeper. He stared at Rachel and Lily squeezed his hand.

"You okay?"

He nodded and pulled her a little closer. *Later.* He decided. *I'll give her some space later. She's just had surgery and a new baby. She truly does need my help.* He rationalized. *After the six weeks are over, I'll put some distance between us.*

Chapter 17

Lily took a deep breath and opened the door. Regina and Charles stood on the doorstep and she smiled at them. "Please, come in."

They crowded into the hallway and Regina gave her a nervous smile. "You're looking good, Lily. How are you feeling?"

"Good. I was a little sore the first few days but it's been nearly two weeks and I'm moving a lot better."

"You're not doing too much, are you?" Regina asked anxiously. "It takes at least a couple of months to heal after surgery."

Lily shook her head. "I've had lots of help. Come into the living room."

Charles cleared his throat. "Is your employer home?"

"He's gone out for a few hours." Lily replied briefly. Logan had taken Hazel out for lunch and a matinee. The little girl was still struggling with accepting Rachel, and both Logan and Lily had been making the effort to give her one-on-one time.

She led her in-laws into the living room. A playpen had been set up in one corner of the room and Rachel was sleeping in it. Regina made a small noise in the back of her throat and hurried over to the playpen. She stared down at the sleeping baby and wiped discreetly at the tears on her cheeks.

"She's so beautiful, Charles." She whispered.

Charles nodded and squeezed her hand as they stared silently at the baby.

"Go ahead and pick her up." Lily said.

Regina glanced at her. "I don't want to wake her."

"You won't."

When Regina continued to hesitate, Lily picked Rachel up. The baby snorted softly but didn't wake and Lily kissed her forehead. "Why don't you have a seat on the couch?"

Regina nodded and she and Charles sat down. Lily placed Rachel in Regina's arms before sitting in the armchair.

"She's so beautiful." Regina repeated. She kissed Rachel's forehead and beamed at Charles. He reached out and stroked the baby's soft skin.

"Thank you for paying the hospital bill. That was very kind of you." Lily said quietly.

"It was the least we could do after how we treated you." Charles said gruffly.

"We're so sorry, Lily. Truly, we are. Thank you for letting us see our granddaughter." Regina said earnestly. "You have no idea how much it means to us."

Lily didn't reply and Regina gave Charles a meaningful look. He cleared his throat again. "Lily, we wanted to," he hesitated, "well, we wanted to offer you the chance to return to yours and Barry's home. We've been talking and we know that how Barry treated you was wrong and he should never have left the house to us. It's yours if you want it. We'll sign it over to you."

Lily stared in shock at Barry's father and he hurried on. "We don't expect anything from you in return. The house should be yours and Rachel's and," he glanced around the room, "it isn't right that you have to live in someone else's home."

"That's very generous of you." Lily said quietly. "I – I'll need to think about it."

"Of course." Regina replied. "Take all the time you need."

She stared at Rachel again. "So, everything's going well with her?"

Lily nodded. "Yes. She's actually, so far, been a very easy baby. I've been really lucky. She eats well and we're already starting to get into a routine."

That routine would change soon, she thought to herself. Despite her protests, she had spent every night in Logan's bed. Each night as soon as Rachel started crying, Logan had appeared in her room. He would urge Lily to crawl into his bed while he carried Rachel to the nursery and changed her.

By the third night, tired of worrying that Hazel would wake when Logan carried the crying Rachel past her room, Lily had taken the baby to Logan's room when they had retired for the night. He had grinned with delight when he saw her standing in his doorway and hurried to bring the bassinet from her room into his.

She couldn't deny that she liked it. Sleeping in Logan's bed, having his warm, hard body pressed firmly against hers, was comforting. It made things easier for her, as well. When Rachel cried, he was out of the bed and picking her up before Lily could even sit up. Most nights she never left the bed. Logan changed Rachel and brought her to Lily for feedings and the one night the baby had been uncharacteristically fussy and out-of-sorts, he had walked her patiently back and forth until she had fallen asleep.

Logan was going back to work tomorrow and while she wasn't nervous about being alone, she was already dreading the thought of sleeping without him. She had grown too accustomed to having him in the bed with her and she sighed softly. They had gone so far past the employer/employee relationship it was ridiculous. Yet, she had no idea if Logan truly cared for her or if he just enjoyed having someone to look after, and she was too afraid to ask. If it was nothing more than his white knight complex, it would crush her.

She sighed again. This morning at three she had fed Rachel and was just drifting back to sleep in Logan's arms when his low voice had drifted out of the darkness.

"I want you to keep sleeping in my room when I'm at work."

She had protested sleepily but he'd shaken his head and pulled her closer against him. "My bed is more comfortable, it's closer to the nursery and besides, Rachel is used to being in here. She won't like it if you go back to your room."

She had laughed and given him a gentle poke. "She won't know the difference, Logan."

"Yes, she will." He replied firmly. "Promise me you'll sleep in my bed while I'm at work."

She had given in quickly and he had smiled with smug satisfaction before burying his face into her neck and falling asleep.

She realized Regina was speaking to her and she gave her an apologetic look. "I'm sorry, what was that?"

"I asked if there was anything you needed." Regina said timidly. "If there were any baby supplies that you were missing or..."

She trailed off and Lily shook her head. "No, Logan is letting me use a lot of Hazel's old baby things so I'm good."

Charles frowned and opened his mouth but Regina elbowed him in the side and gave him a pointed look. He closed his mouth with a snap and Regina smiled at Lily. "Well, if you need anything just let us know, alright? We'd be happy to help."

* * *

"I swear every time I see her, she's grown." Janet plucked Rachel from Lily's arms and kissed her smooth cheek. "I can't believe she's nearly six weeks old, already."

Rachel stared at her before a wide grin broke out across her face.

"She's smiling!" Janet said delightedly.

"Isn't it adorable?" Lily grinned before helping Hazel out of her boots and jacket. She kissed the little girl's head fondly.

"Baby bug, do you want to play with Nicole or do you want to stay with me?"

"I'll play with Nicole." Hazel replied.

"She's downstairs, honey." Janet opened the fridge door. "Do you want a juice box to take with you?"

"Yes, please." Hazel took the offered juice box and hesitated. "You won't leave without me, right mommy?"

Lily shook her head. "Of course not, honey. I'll be right here in the kitchen if you need me."

Hazel left the room and Janet raised her eyebrows at Lily. "She's calling you mommy now?"

Lily flushed. "She started doing it a few days after I came home with Rachel. I corrected her the first few times but she just ignored me. I asked Logan to speak to her about it and he did but she still does it."

She gave Janet a hesitant look. "I'm not trying to replace Erin or anything."

Janet rolled her eyes. "Honey, Erin was a shit mother and everyone knows it. Hazel deserves to have a mother like you."

"I'm not her mom though. I'm her nanny." Lily said quietly. "In a year, Hazel will be in school and I'll be out of a job. It isn't right that I let her call me mommy, I know that, but I love her and she's been having a hard time adjusting to the new baby. I don't want to make it worse."

Janet jiggled Rachel gently and kissed her chubby cheeks. "Have you and Logan talked about your feelings for each other?"

Lily shook her head. "No, but last night in bed, he – "

"Whoa. In bed?" Janet grinned at Lily.

Lily blushed. "Logan's room is closer to the nursery and his bed is more comfortable and, as weird as this sounds, he really seems to enjoy helping with Rachel in the night. I tried to tell him he didn't need to help but if I don't stay in his room, he shows up in mine the minute Rachel starts crying and carries her to his room. I finally just gave up."

She cleared her throat. "We're not uh, having sex or anything like that. It's just easier with the baby."

"Oh I know, honey. You have to wait the six weeks to have sex." Janet said cheerfully. "But just think – when the six weeks are done, it'll be much easier to sex Logan up if you're in his bed."

Lily turned bright red and Janet laughed. "Although I still think you should have taken my advice and slept with him while you were pregnant. I cannot emphasize enough how amazing your orgasms are when…"

She trailed off and stared thoughtfully at Lily. Lily bit at her lip and dropped her gaze to the table as a wide grin crossed Janet's face.

"Holy shit! You had sex with him. Didn't you?"

Lily didn't reply and Janet reached out and poked her. "Spill your guts, girl."

"We had sex the night before Rachel was born. I was so tired of being pregnant, and so I started walking up and down the stairs to try and induce labour and Logan heard me. He came out of his room half-naked, and I almost had a damn orgasm right there. All I could think about was how much I wanted him and how you said sex could bring labour on." The words spilled out of her in a rush.

"And then I touched him, just his chest, but he got this look on his face and then I might have said something about sex bringing on labour and he might have said something about being happy to help."

She glanced up at Janet. "The next thing I knew, I was naked in his bed and riding him like he was a damn pony."

She blushed at her own boldness as Janet laughed again. "Awesome! And? Pregnancy sex is amazing. Am I right?"

Lily nodded. "Yes. It was unbelievable. I couldn't get enough of him and I was kind of demanding and stuff. Poor Logan."

Janet rolled her eyes. "Oh yes, poor Logan."

"I made him have sex with me five times that night." Lily said with embarrassment. "I think back to that night and I'm so mortified. He would start to drift off to sleep and then I'd wake him up again. He probably thinks I'm some sort of nymphomaniac."

Rachel gave a short disgruntled cry and Janet stood and paced back and forth, jiggling her lightly. "Five times. Christ, no wonder your water broke the next day."

She laughed and kissed Rachel's chubby cheeks. "So, are you going to sleep with him again?"

"I don't know." Lily confessed. "I told him it could only be a one-time thing, that I just wanted to bring on labour, and he agreed. He hasn't made any uh, moves on me or anything like that since Rachel was born."

She sighed. "I think he's lost interest."

"He hasn't." Janet said immediately. "Logan's not stupid. He's not going to ask you to sleep with him before you've healed from the C-section. I guarantee you – he'll be all over you the minute those six weeks are up."

Lily shook her head. "He's been sleeping in the same bed with me for weeks and he hasn't had, I mean, there's no uh indication that he wants me." She blushed again as Janet shrugged.

"Just because Logan can keep from getting a stiffy when you're in the bed with him, doesn't mean he isn't interested, Lily."

Lily gaped at her. "Janet!"

Janet shrugged. "You know I'm right."

"Now," she switched Rachel to the other arm and cooed at the baby before glancing at Lily, "I've been meaning to ask if you've let Barry's parents meet Rachel yet."

Lily nodded. "I have. They've been over a few times when Logan's out with Hazel."

"Does Logan know?"

She shook her head. "No. He doesn't want them seeing her and I understand why but I really think they've changed, Janet. They paid the hospital bill and offered to give me the house that Barry and I lived in, no strings attached."

"Wow. Are you going to take it?" Janet asked.

Lily shrugged. "I don't know. Even if I did, there's still the matter of my job. I need to live with Logan in order to look after Hazel and besides, I don't have many fond memories of that house. Logan's house has been more of a home to me than that one ever was. But I'm going to need someplace to live once Hazel is in school and I'm out of a job. I believe that this is an honest gift from Regina and Charles and that they truly just want to be a part of Rachel's life."

"Then that's what matters." Janet said firmly. "Logan means well but, at the end of the day, you're Rachel's mother and you need to do what you think is best for her."

"Thanks, Janet. I just – I hate lying to Logan."

"I know, honey." Janet said sympathetically. "Sooner or later you're going to have to talk to him about it but for now, just concentrate on Rachel and Hazel and figuring out how you feel about Logan. If you love him, you need to tell him."

"I know." Lily answered quietly.

Chapter 18

Logan stared up at the ceiling of his bedroom. Lily was lying beside him and he wondered if she'd fallen asleep. Rachel had been sleeping for nearly an hour and he shifted in the bed and sighed quietly.

She had turned six weeks old two days ago and Lily had started placing her in her crib at night. She, however, had continued to sleep in his bed and although he was thrilled about that, a small part of him found her presence torturous. Over the last few weeks it had grown increasingly difficult to hide his arousal from her whenever they were in the bed together.

Lily turned to face him and he studied her face in the dim light. She was absolutely gorgeous and he let his eyes drift to her breasts. She was wearing a thin nightshirt and his cock hardened as he thought about cupping her breasts. He closed his eyes, remembering the way she had moaned and cried out when he had slid into her. She had been soft and warm, and he bit back his groan of frustration and balled his hands into fists. He had to stop thinking about her. Had to stop thinking about reaching over and stroking her soft skin. If he didn't, he would –

"Logan?"

He jumped and cleared his throat. "Yes?" His voice was hoarse with need and he cleared his throat again.

"What's wrong?"

"Nothing's wrong." He muttered.

"There is." She insisted. She slid over to his side of the bed before he could stop her. "You normally lie right beside me. Why are you so far – "

She stopped, her cheeks turning pink, when she felt his erection pressing against her stomach. He groaned and turned away from her.

"I'm sorry, Lily."

She didn't reply and he shifted the blankets back. "I'll sleep in your room tonight."

Her hand wrapped around his arm and she pushed him back down before pressing her body against his back and ass. He groaned again when she rubbed his chest.

"I don't want you to go." She whispered.

"Lily, I think it's better if I – "

His words turned into a drawn out hiss of pleasure as Lily's hand slipped past the waistband of his boxers, and her long fingers curled around his throbbing cock. She stroked him firmly before placing a soft kiss on his naked back.

"Don't leave me, Logan."

"Christ, Lily." He moaned as she tightened her hand around him and rubbed slowly back and forth.

"Lie on your back, honey." She whispered.

He shifted on to his back and she pulled the covers down before reaching for his boxers. He lifted his hips and helped her push them off his legs before she dipped her head and placed a soft kiss on his abdomen.

He shuddered beneath her mouth and she smiled before placing a series of soft kisses down his stomach. She dipped her tongue into his navel and he groaned loudly. "Please, sweetheart."

She smiled again and moved until her mouth was hovering over his erect cock. She sucked just the head of it into her mouth and traced it with her tongue. Logan cried out, his hips thrusting upwards as his hand curled into her long hair.

"Oh, please." He moaned again.

She slid her mouth down his erection and sucked. He was panting and twisting below her and he whispered her name as she hollowed her cheeks and sucked firmly before releasing him. She gripped the base of his cock, moisture was pooling between her thighs and her entire body was throbbing for release, and licked him slowly, concentrating on the sensitive ridge around the head before sucking on just the head again.

When he was shuddering uncontrollably and his breath coming in harsh pants, she kissed her way back up his body. Her mouth found his ear and she swept her tongue along the edge of his ear before whispering, "Make love to me, Logan."

He cupped her face and stared intently at her before nodding. She stripped her nightshirt off and wriggled out of her panties as he took a condom from the bedside table and hurriedly rolled it onto his cock.

She parted her thighs and urged him between them. He gave her a worried look. "Lily, are you sure it's okay? I don't want to hurt you."

"You won't." She whispered. She cupped his face and tugged until she could place a gentle kiss on his mouth.

He kissed her back, thrusting his tongue into her mouth as he slid deep inside of her. She moaned, her muscles tightening around him in exquisite pleasure as he continued to kiss her and cupped one full breast. He rubbed her nipple with his thumb as he slowly pushed in and out of her.

She gripped his waist and met each of his thrusts as they kissed hungrily. Her entire body pulsed with pleasure and need, and she couldn't stop the small moans and whimpers as he continued the same, slow pace. She nipped at his bottom lip and he inhaled sharply before thrusting roughly in and out of her.

"So good." She murmured against his mouth. She wrapped her legs around his waist, locking her feet together behind his back and dug her nails into his broad back. He was starting to lose the steady rhythm he had set and she welcomed it, urging him to go faster with hard thrusts of her hips.

Their bodies slapped against each other in a quickening rhythm, their breathing harsh and loud in the quiet night. Lily buried her face in Logan's neck, her body stiffening and her pussy squeezing his cock in a hot, tight grip, as her orgasm rushed through her.

Logan groaned and thrust rapidly before arching his back and muttering her name in a harsh whisper. He shuddered above her, the tendons in his neck standing out, as he came and then dropped gently on to her warm body.

She kissed his neck and stroked his warm back.

"Am I hurting you?" He mumbled.

"No." She whispered. She kept her legs locked tightly around him as his cock softened inside of her. He nuzzled her throat and rubbed her side before finally rolling off of her. She curled up on her side as he disposed of the condom before turning to face her.

She wrapped them both in the blanket, pressing her entire body against his as he smiled at her. "That was amazing, sweetheart."

She smiled happily. "It really was."

He laughed and pulled her closer, dropping a kiss on her forehead. "Go to sleep, sweetheart. We have about three hours before the baby bee will be wanting her midnight snack."

Lily closed her eyes and rested her head against Logan's chest. She knew they needed to talk about what was happening between them but the lovemaking had left her warm and sleepy.

Tomorrow, she decided, *I'll sit Logan down tomorrow and tell him I think I'm falling in love with him.*

* * *

"Lily? Are you alright today? You're quiet." Regina touched her shoulder and Lily forced herself to smile at the older woman.

Last night, lying in Logan's arms, it had seemed like an easy decision to tell him that she loved him. This morning though, harsh reality had set in and she had chickened out. If he didn't love her, she would have an entire year to live with him in utter humiliation.

No you wouldn't. Her inner voice whispered insidiously. *If you tell Logan you love him and he doesn't feel the same, he'll either encourage you to find a new job or outright fire you.*

He wouldn't, she argued back. He's not that kind of man.

Maybe not. But do you really want to live and work for a man who is perfectly happy to fuck you senseless, but doesn't love you? Have some pride, girl.

She shut out her inner voice and made herself smile at Regina again. "I'm fine, Regina. Just a little tired today."

Regina glanced at the couch where Charles was holding Rachel. He was making silly faces at the baby and Lily felt a smile crossing her lips, despite her worry. Rachel had thrown up all over him not twenty minutes ago and she could see the large damp stain on the front of his, no doubt, expensive designer shirt. She had apologized profusely but Charles had waved it off and refused to give Rachel back. She never thought she would see the day where Barry's father, always so cold and distant, would be covered in baby vomit and be perfectly content with it.

"Did Rachel keep you up?"

Lily shook her head. "No. She was only up once last night."

"Wow, that's great!" Regina said happily. "Barry was still waking up two or three times a night when he was eight months old. I would have sold my soul for one good night's sleep."

Her smile faltered and she scrubbed at her eyes quickly. Lily gave her a sympathetic look and touched her arm gently. "I'm sorry, Regina. I know you miss him."

"I do." She said hoarsely. "I know he wasn't the – the best boy, but he was still my boy and I loved him so."

Lily nodded as Regina turned to stare at Rachel again. "I know we keep saying this, Lily, but we're so happy to be a part of Rachel's life. Thank you."

"You're welcome." Lily said softly. She discreetly glanced at her watch. Logan had taken Hazel to an indoor play area for kids, and she wanted to make sure that Regina and Charles were gone before they got back. It was nearly three and Logan had said they would be back by four. She had plenty of time to –

She heard the front door open and slam shut and she froze with surprise when Hazel, still wearing her jacket and boots, ran into the living room.

"Mommy! My tummy hurts and I can't stop pooping!" She wailed loudly. "Daddy said you would cuddle me in bed. Will you – "

She stopped in the middle of the room and stared curiously at Regina and Charles. "Who are you?"

"Hazel, honey, this is – "

Before Lily could finish, Logan popped his head into the living room. "Hazel, come take your boots and jacket…"

He trailed off, staring in surprise at Regina before his gaze fell on Charles holding Rachel. Anger crossed his face and he strode jerkily into the room. "What are you doing here?"

Without waiting for a reply, he stalked across the room to Charles and held his arms out. "Give her to me."

Charles frowned and held Rachel a little closer. "Who do you think you are? This is my grandchild and I'll not be told to just hand her over."

"Give her to me, now." Logan repeated quietly.

Lily hurried over and stood between them. She took Rachel from Charles and tugged on Logan's arm, pulling him away from her father-in-law.

"Hazel, run upstairs to your room, okay? I'll be right up with some medicine for your stomach and to cuddle with you."

"I want to stay with you." Hazel whispered. She stared anxiously at her father before leaning against Lily and putting her thin arm around Lily's leg. "Mommy, why is daddy mad?"

"I'm not mad, baby bug." Logan said without looking at her. "Listen to Lily, please."

He folded his arms across his chest and glared at Charles and Regina as Hazel gave Lily a pleading look.

"Come upstairs with me. Please, mommy."

Lily crouched down and kissed Hazel's cheek as the little girl rubbed Rachel's head. "I'll be right up, baby bug. I promise. Take your boots off before you go upstairs, okay?"

"Okay." The little girl sighed and left the room. Lily waited until she heard the little girl going up the stairs before she crossed the room to Logan. He was giving her a wounded look and she sighed softly.

"Logan, don't look at me like that. They're her grandparents. They deserve the right to see her."

Rachel made a cry of discomfort and Lily raised her to her shoulder. Before she could pat her back, Logan took the baby from her and rested her against one broad shoulder. He rubbed and patted her back as, completely ignoring Lily and her in-laws, he paced back and forth. Rachel quieted almost immediately and made a soft sound of contentment before burping loudly.

"That's my good baby bee." Logan whispered to her. His body was still stiff with anger and Lily turned to Regina and Charles.

"I think you should go. I'll call you in a day or two and – "

"Are you sure he should be around the baby when he's that angry?" Charles asked loudly. "I don't trust that he won't hurt her."

Lily's temper flared and she turned on the older man. "Logan would never hurt Rachel! Don't you dare suggest that he would! He loves her. Do you understand?"

Regina made a soothing motion with her hands. "Of course, Lily. Charles didn't mean that. He's just protective of Rachel."

"All I'm saying is that you don't really know this man." Charles said heatedly.

"You're living in his home, taking care of his daughter who's calling you *mommy*," he gave her a look of disbelief, "and he's acting like my grandchild, Barry's daughter, is his."

He turned to Logan. "She's not yours. You do understand that you don't you? My grandchild is not *your* child and you have no right to keep us from seeing her. You're not even –

"Charles!" Lily snapped at him. "Enough! You can't – "

"Get out of my house." Logan said calmly.

Lily glanced at him. He was still angry, she could almost see it radiating from him, but he was holding Rachel gently and staring fixedly at Charles.

"I will do no such thing!" Charles protested. "I have every right to see my grandchild and – "

"Get out of my house." Logan said slowly and deliberately. "I won't ask you again."

"Let's go, Charles." Regina said sharply. She gathered her coat and gave Lily an anxious look. "Call us later. Please, Lily."

She pulled her husband out of the living room, he was giving Logan a dark look of anger, and Lily followed them to the front door.

"Lily, will you be okay?" Regina asked hesitantly.

"Yes. Logan is a good man, and he would never hurt Rachel or me. I'll call you later." Lily replied firmly as she opened the front door.

When they had left, she took a deep breath and shut the door before returning to the living room. Logan was standing at the window, still holding Rachel, and he gave her another look of hurt.

"You lied to me, Lily."

"I didn't." She said calmly.

"You didn't tell me that you were letting them see Rachel. That – that you were letting them come to my house."

"I'm sorry that I invited them to your house. I knew you didn't want them here and it was wrong of me to go behind your back like that. I should have taken Rachel to their home." She replied quietly.

He gave her an angry look. "They don't deserve to see her. Why can't you understand that? They would take her from us in a heartbeat if they had the chance."

"They wouldn't." She shook her head. "They just want to be a part of her life, Logan. And they deserve the chance to fix what they did."

He snorted loudly. "No, they don't. Their son was terrible to you and they were just as terrible. They kicked you out of your own home, for God's sake! You would have been homeless if it hadn't been for me. Have you forgotten that?"

"No." She said evenly. "I haven't forgotten and you know how grateful I am to you. But they really are trying. They've offered to sign over the house to me. They said – "

"At what price?" He interrupted. "They're suddenly so willing to give you what was rightfully yours all along because why?"

"Because they know what Barry did was wrong. Because they – "

"Because they want Rachel and you under their thumbs!" He suddenly shouted. Rachel, who had been starting to fall asleep against his chest, gave a startled cry.

He took a deep breath and rubbed her back soothingly, as he swayed back and forth. "They're trying to control you, Lily. Just like Barry did." He said quietly.

"No, they're not." She tried to keep her temper in check. "Logan, you have to trust that I have Rachel's best interests at heart. I'm not – "

"I don't want them seeing her. I don't trust them and sooner or later they're going to prove me right. You're too naïve to see that, Lily. You're too – too trusting and sweet to understand what people like them are really like." He interrupted again.

"I'm not stupid, Logan." She said tightly. She was starting to get angry and she tried to swallow it down, to keep her cool, as Logan glared at her.

"I never said you were. What I said was that you're too naïve. These people will eat you alive and take Rachel the first chance they get!"

"Stop it!" She said furiously. "I understand that you care about Rachel and want what's best for her, but I'm her mother. I make the decisions about what's best for her."

"They're not going near our baby!" He shouted again. "That's final, Lily!"

Rachel began to cry loudly and Lily stalked to Logan and held her hands out. "She's not our baby, Logan. She's my baby. Give her to me."

He closed his eyes and then kissed Rachel's face before handing her to Lily. She soothed the baby quickly, rubbing her back and patting her bottom as the baby rested her head on her chest.

"As long as you and Rachel are living here, those people are not to see her. Do you understand, Lily?" He said angrily.

She gave him a look of astonishment. "I am not your – your child, Logan. You don't get to just tell me what I can and can't do. You're my employer, nothing else, and I make the decisions concerning my child. Do you understand *that*?"

"I'm more than your employer and you know it!" He snapped. "And after everything I've done for you, I think I have the right to voice my opinion on who gets to see Rachel. You owe me that."

She froze and gave him a look of such shock and hurt that his anger faded. He reached out for her, his blood growing cold, when she backed away.

"I'm sorry, Lily." He said hoarsely. "I didn't mean that. I just – I care about you and Rachel and I don't want – "

"This isn't working, Logan." She said in a toneless little voice. "I think it would be better for both of us if I quit and move out. I won't live with someone who thinks they can tell me what to do, or believes that their kindness to me means I owe them a debt. I spent too many years living under Barry's rules and believing that I couldn't stand on my own two feet. I won't do it again."

He swallowed thickly. "That isn't what I'm doing."

"It is." She said calmly. "You know it is. Thank you for everything you've done but Rachel and I are leaving in the morning."

"Hazel." He said desperately. "You'll break her heart if you leave, Lily."

She pressed her lips together as tears started to flow down her cheeks. "Don't, Logan. Don't you dare use Hazel as some kind of bargaining chip. You'll be no better than Charles and Regina, if you do."

"Lily, I – "

She shook her head. "No, we're done. I'll pack tonight and talk with Hazel in the morning."

She turned and left the room, leaving Logan to stare miserably after her.

Chapter 19

"You look like shit, man." Rob said gravely.

"Yeah, thanks." Logan scrubbed his hand across his beard and gave Rob a dirty look.

Rob shrugged and dropped down on the couch beside him. "Have you got any sleep since Lily left?"

"A bit." Logan muttered.

"It's been two weeks, dude. If you don't start getting it together, Bill's going to make you take a leave of absence."

Rob glanced across the common room at Bill who was sitting at the table and reading the paper. "You need to go to Lily and beg for her forgiveness."

Logan shook his head. "It's too late. I was an asshole and acted like her goddamn dead husband. She'll never forgive me for that."

"You might be surprised." Rob said gently. "I'm sure she's miserable without you."

Logan snorted. "Yes, I'm sure it's terrible for her to be living in that giant mansion, with Charles and Regina to take care of her every need."

Rob punched him hard on the shoulder. "You're being an asshole again. Lily's been talking to Janet and they've been really good to her. I don't know the entire story about why you hate them so much, but Janet was visiting

Lily when they stopped by and she said they seemed pretty nice. They obviously care about Rachel and they seem to be respectful of Lily."

Logan glared at him and then sighed loudly. "Fuck. I know. I overreacted but I was worried they would try and take Rachel from us."

Rob glanced at his watch. "Your shift is over. Janet said to tell you that she'll watch Hazel overnight if you want to, you know, go to Lily and beg for forgiveness."

"I really appreciate Janet looking after Hazel for me. She knows that right?" Logan said.

"She does." Rob confirmed. "Any lucky in finding a new nanny yet?"

"No." Logan couldn't tell him that he hadn't even started looking for one. He couldn't bring himself to look for a woman to replace Lily. She had been perfect and he had let her slip away because of his own stupidity.

He rubbed his face again. "Did Hazel have a good day?"

"She did." Rob answered. "She's been a perfect angel for Janet."

Logan shook his head in confusion. "I don't understand it. Hazel – well – she flipped out when Lily left."

He shuddered, remembering the look on Lily's face when Hazel had screamed and cried and threw a tantrum. She had thrown herself at Lily, pounding at her with her tiny fists as Lily tried vainly to soothe her.

"You promised you'd never leave me!" She had screamed repeatedly. Logan had finally pulled Hazel away from Lily, holding on to his little girl grimly as she flailed and screamed herself hoarse.

Lily, sobbing heartbreakingly and clutching Rachel's car seat in a death grip, had fled the house to the waiting cab. Later that afternoon, after Hazel had cried herself to sleep, a man in a silver car had pulled into his driveway. He had identified himself as an employee of Charles and Regina, and Logan had watched numbly as the man took the large, packed suitcase from Lily's room and left.

She had left nearly all of Hazel's borrowed baby things behind. He had walked into the empty, silent nursery and sat heavily in the rocking chair. Two hours later, Hazel had crept into the room and crawled into his lap. He rocked her like he had when she was a baby and said soft, meaningless words of comfort as she sobbed quietly.

He had done his best over the next couple of days to act cheerful around Hazel and to make her happy but the little girl had been sullen and withdrawn. He was nearly paralyzed with worry when he dropped her off with Janet on his first day back at work. She had hugged the crying little girl and assured Logan she would be fine. Knowing she was wrong, he was thrown for a loop when he'd called later that night and talked with Hazel. She had been cheerful and happy and some of the guilt and worry had lifted a little. When he picked her up three days later, she was completely back to her old self. He didn't understand it but he hadn't questioned it, just filled with relief that she seemed to be coping with Lily's absence.

Now, he gave Rob a look of confusion. "I just don't get it. She was devastated when Lily left but the last week or so she's been happy and normal."

"Kids, man. They're resilient, you know?" Rob was giving him an oddly guilty look but before Logan could question him about it, the alarm went off with a shrill bray.

Rob jumped to his feet and clapped Logan on the back. "Go home before Bill makes you go on the call."

Logan nodded and watched as Rob hurried out of the room. Within minutes, the previously busy fire house was nearly empty and he stood up as the loud siren of the truck started. He wandered downstairs and stood in the silence for a moment before heading toward dispatch.

He was done his shift and he should be leaving to pick up Hazel and going home but he didn't want to. He didn't want to go home to his empty house. He didn't want to smile and pretend to Hazel that everything was okay without Lily and Rachel.

He sighed harshly and stuck his head into the dispatcher's room. "Hey Judy. How are you?"

"Good." The young woman smiled at him. "Aren't you done your shift?"

"Yeah." He leaned against her desk and watched as she typed something into her computer. "What was the call for?"

"House fire." She said absently. "Some place over in the ritzy part of town. Downing Street, I think."

Logan's blood ran cold. "Downing Street? Are you sure?" He asked hoarsely.

She gave him an odd look. "Yes. Why?"

"What's the address?" He had only been to Lily's former house once before but he remembered the address easily enough.

"Um, I'm not sure." She replied.

"Check!" He nearly shouted at her and she gave him a startled look before hunching over her computer.

"Eleven. Eleven Downing Street." She glanced up at Logan. "Logan? What's wrong?"

Logan turned and bolted from the office.

* * *

The house was fully engulfed in flames when he drove up. He jumped out of his car, staring in horror at the bright orange flames, and staggered toward the house. His coworkers were hosing the house down with a grim sort of determinedness but even he could see it was a losing battle.

Charles and Regina were standing on the sidewalk, their arms around each other like two lost children, and he lurched toward them. He grabbed Regina's arm, his face mad with panic and fear, and shook her roughly.

"Is Lily home?" He shouted. "Are her and the baby at home?"

"We- we're not sure." Regina sobbed. "The neighbours called us and we came right over. They – they tried to get into the house but it was already too dangerous. They think that Lily and Rachel are in there." She gave him a look of stark fear as Logan turned and stared in horror at the burning house.

"LILY!" He screamed her name and ran toward the house. He had to get in there, he had to find her and Rachel and –

He was tackled and knocked to the ground as he raced up the sidewalk leading to the house. He fought bitterly against the man holding him down and screamed Lily's name again. Rob, his head and face covered by a helmet and mask, shook him roughly before ripping his mask off.

"Logan! Stop it! She's not – "

"It's not too late!" Logan shouted at him. "I can save her! Get off me!"

Rob struggled to pin him down. "Listen to me, Logan! She's not – "

His head flew back with a snap when Logan punched him hard in the jaw. The blow knocked him over and he shook his head dazedly as Logan staggered to his feet.

"LILY!" He screamed again. He started toward the house. His panic and need to find her were so great that he almost didn't hear her call his name. The small part of him that wasn't being controlled by his panic forced him to a stop. He whirled around, his jaw dropping open when he saw Lily standing on the sidewalk.

"Logan!" She cried and he stumbled to her. He stared down at her and touched her cheek with one trembling finger.

"You weren't in there." He whispered.

She shook her head no and he felt another overwhelming moment of fear when he saw her empty arms. "Rachel! Where's Rachel?"

"She's fine. She's safe, honey. She's with Janet." Lily said soothingly.

He stared blankly at her and she reached up and cupped his face. "We're okay, honey."

He threw his arms around her and lifted her up, smothering her face with kisses. "I'm so sorry, Lily. Please come home. I love you." He kissed her hard on the mouth. "I love you so much."

Crying, she kissed him back before resting her forehead against his. "I love you too, Logan."

He hugged her tightly and she rubbed his back as Regina and Charles approached them. "It's alright, honey. Put me down, okay?"

He nodded and set her on her feet, holding her hand tightly as she smiled at Regina and Charles.

"Oh, Lily." Regina whispered. Her face was white and she was clutching compulsively at the collar of her jacket. "Oh, Lily." She repeated.

"We're fine." Lily tugged her way free of Logan's grip and hugged Regina briefly before squeezing Charles' arm. She looked at the burning house with sorrow as Logan pulled her back into his arms.

"I'm so sorry about your house." She said to Regina and Charles. "I know I didn't leave anything on. I don't – "

Charles shook his head. "We don't care about the house, Lily. We're just glad you and Rachel are safe."

She nodded as Charles hesitated and then held his hand out to Logan. "I'm sorry. It's obvious how much you love Lily and Rachel."

Logan shook his hand. "I'm sorry as well."

Regina touched Lily's arm. "You're welcome to stay at our house tonight. We don't have a crib but we've got plenty of room for you and Rachel."

Lily shook her head. "Thank you but we're going home with Logan."

Logan hugged her closer as Rob approached them. He was rubbing his jaw and he gave Logan a dry look.

"Sorry, man." Logan said apologetically.

"Yeah, don't mention it." He glanced behind him at the burning house. "I'm sorry, Lily. We weren't able to get anything out of the house. It was too dangerous."

"That's alright." Lily replied softly. "Thank you for trying."

Logan stared down at her. "Why is Rachel with Janet?" He asked suddenly

Lily flushed a little. "I've been um, visiting Hazel whenever you brought her to Janet's."

Logan didn't reply and she hurried on. "Please don't be angry, Logan. I just missed her so much and I couldn't stand the thought of never seeing her again. I asked Rob and Janet not to say anything and," she gave him an embarrassed look, "I encouraged Hazel to keep it a secret as well."

He shook his head. "I'm not angry, Lily. I love that you love Hazel so much."

She gave him a smile of relief as he frowned. "How did you know the house was on fire?"

"I called home on my way to the fire." Rob chimed in. "I knew Lily lived on Downing Street and I wanted to check that she was still safe at our house and confirm her actual address."

"I was just about to leave when Rob called." Lily said. "I knew you would be there soon to pick up Hazel, and I didn't want to risk running into you. When I found out the house was on fire, I left Rachel with Janet and drove over here."

She squeezed Logan's hand. "How did you know?"

I checked in with dispatch before I left. When I realized it was your house I panicked." He hugged her again. "I was so afraid I was going to lose you, Lily. I don't ever want to feel that way again. I love you."

She smiled sweetly at him. "I love you too, Logan."

EPILOGUE

"Happy Anniversary, sweetheart." Logan appeared in the kitchen, a huge bouquet of flowers in his hands.

Lily stared at him in surprise. "You're home early from work."

He grinned. "I am. Bill told me to go home and spend some time with my beautiful wife on our one-year anniversary."

She laughed and kissed him firmly on the mouth. "How nice of him." She admired the flowers in his hand. "These are lovely."

"Lovely flowers for a lovely girl." He winked at her and set the flowers on the counter. "Is the baby bee sleeping?"

"She is. She was in a real mood this morning." Lily laughed again.

"Hmm." Logan gave her a thoughtful look. "The baby bee is sleeping and Hazel won't be finished school for another couple of hours. What should we do with so much unexpected alone time?"

Lily grinned at him. "I'm sure you can think of something."

"I certainly can." He cupped her breast and kissed her softly. "In fact, I – "

He stopped, a small smile crossing his face, and rested his hand on Lily's round belly. "Someone's active."

Lily placed her hand on top of his. "Your son has been kicking rather enthusiastically all morning."

He bent and kissed her belly. "Hello, little man." He smiled again when Lily's belly rippled under his hand. "I can't wait to meet you."

END

Please enjoy a sample chapter of Elizabeth Kelly's latest novel, "Saving Charlotte".

SAVING CHARLOTTE

By Elizabeth Kelly

* * * *

Chapter 1

"How are Melody and the kids?" Charlotte turned the clippers on and began to carefully shave the back of Vince's neck.

"They're good, real good." Vince smiled at her in the mirror as she finished shaving his neck and brushed away the small bits of hair that still clung to his sunburned neck.

"Jade's leaving for college next week."

Charlotte shook her head in disbelief. "I can't believe she's starting college this year."

"You and me both." Vince grimaced a little. "And why she feels the need to move halfway across the country is beyond me."

"Mel is going to miss her." Charlotte replied.

Vince sighed heavily. "Yeah, she really will."

"At least you still have Daniel at home."

"True." Vince acknowledged. "Although this is his last year of high school, and I imagine he'll choose a college as far away from here as he can get too."

"This is a small city. Kids are always eager to leave."

"Yeah, but I had hoped that one of them might follow their old man's career path."

Charlotte smiled gently at him. "Jade is going into criminology is she not?"

He nodded. "Yeah, but it ain't the same as being a cop. We both know she'll become a lawyer like her mother. And Daniel is planning on majoring in theatre. Theatre! Tell me, what kind of job will the kid get from that?"

Before Charlotte could reply, Vince sighed. "Mel says kids need to follow their own path and we need to encourage Daniel to follow his dreams. I don't disagree, but we'll see how she feels when Danny's thirty-eight and living in our basement."

Charlotte laughed and Vince grinned at her in the mirror. "It's good to hear you laugh, Charlotte. Mel and I have been worried about you."

"I'm fine, Vince."

He grunted and shifted in the chair before glancing around the salon. The other two hair stylists were chatting in the back of the salon and Carmen, the receptionist, was on the phone booking an appointment.

"I doubt you're fine." He said gently. "It's only been three months."

"True." Charlotte replied as she swept the bits of iron-grey hair from his cape-covered shoulders. "But he was sick for nearly two years before that. It gives a person time to prepare."

"I know." He drew his hand free from the cape and placed it on top of hers. "It doesn't mean you're not lonely though."

"No, it doesn't." Charlotte admitted. "But there's relief in knowing he isn't suffering anymore."

She squeezed Vince's hand briefly before unbuttoning the cape and carefully shaking it out. "Are you heading home now?"

He shook his head. "Nah. I'm working late tonight. We've been having some trouble with a motorcycle gang that showed up a couple of months ago. We suspect they've been trafficking and dealing in drugs. As if we don't have enough trouble with that already."

He eased his body out of the chair and straightened his uniform before placing his police cap back on his head. Charlotte followed him to the reception, leaning against the counter as Vince paid Carmen. He left her a generous tip as usual, and she smiled gratefully at him.

"Why don't you come by this weekend? I know Mel would love to see you again." Vince asked as he slid his wallet into his back pocket.

"That sounds nice. Tell Mel to text me." Charlotte answered.

Vince hesitated and then gave her a brief but firm hug. "And you know if you need anything, anything at all, you can just call us right?"

"I know, Vince. Thank you."

He nodded and left the salon as Charlotte returned to her station to sweep up the bits of hair on the floor around her chair. Her back hurt and she had the beginning of a headache, but she thought she had done an admirable job of convincing Vince that she was fine.

She sighed. It wasn't that she wasn't fine, she decided. She wasn't anything. She felt no overwhelming sadness or loneliness, nor did she feel happiness or joy. The morning after Rick had died, she had woken to discover a curious sort of numbness had swallowed her every emotion as neatly as the whale had swallowed Jonah. She had hidden it well from her friends and family; only her therapist knew about her sudden inability to feel anything at all. She didn't believe she was suicidal, but she also couldn't deny that the thought of her own death brought only a weary kind of relief.

She swallowed hard, trying to force herself into feeling some kind of terror or even discomfort at the idea of her very existence fading out like a dying candle, but there was only the numbness. As she swept at the tiled floor, she sighed again. There was no point in trying to force herself to feel something she didn't. She had to work through the grief just like her therapist kept telling her. This lack of emotion, this numbness, was just a cleverly masqueraded stage of grief – it would pass eventually.

Her head swivelled towards the front door of the salon as the loud pop of firecrackers came from outside. She wandered towards reception as Darlene stood up from behind her desk.

"Did you hear that?"

Charlotte nodded. "Weird to have firecrackers this time of the year."

"I don't think it was firecrackers." Darlene hesitated. "It sounded like gunfire to me. Maybe you shouldn't go out there Charlotte."

Charlotte who was pushing open the front door, glanced over her shoulder at the young woman. "I'm just going to check – "

She gasped as Vince, his face pale and his hand pressed against his side, staggered through the open door.

"Charlotte, lock the door." He wheezed. He suddenly toppled over, knocking her off her feet. She gasped with pain as she fell to the floor, her elbow slamming painfully into the hard tile. With a grunt of effort, she pushed Vince off of her and on to his back as Rita and Helen hurried over from the back of the salon.

"Vince?" She stared in disbelief at the bright bloom of blood seeping through the front of Vince's shirt.

"Charlotte," he groaned, "the door – quick."

Before she could gain her feet, the bell over the door rang out and three men entered the salon. All three were dressed similarly in dirty jeans, white t-shirts and leather vests. The first man had a gun in his hand and Vince's gun shoved into the front of his pants, and he pointed the gun in his hand at Darlene.

"Lock the door - now."

She stared frozen at him and he slapped her across the head. "Now, bitch!"

She stumbled to the door and locked it as the second man pulled the shade down over the large picture window. He moved to the door, shoving Darlene out of the way and turned the open sign to close before pulling the shade on the door as well.

The third man, he was tall and broad with long dark hair tied back in a ponytail and a thick beard covering his face, grabbed a stack of towels from Rita's station and knelt beside Vince. He pressed two of the towels to the gunshot on Vince's side and grabbed Charlotte's hand.

"Apply pressure." He growled to her, pressing her hand down hard on the towels. She did as he asked as he leaned over Vince and felt for his pulse in his neck.

"Hang on, old man." He breathed so quietly that only Charlotte and Vince heard him. Charlotte looked at Vince. He was staring at the man above him, and Charlotte could have sworn that a flicker of recognition crossed Vince's face.

"What the fuck are you doing, Ren? Leave him!" The first man snapped.

The man named Ren stared at Charlotte for a moment, his dark grey eyes assessing her coolly. "Don't let up on the pressure. Do you hear me?"

She nodded as he stood and moved back to the other two men.

"What the hell, Ren? Who gives a shit about that old fart?"

Ren glared at the smaller man. "Do you want to add murder to your list of crimes, Steve? Killing a cop will get you the chair, you moron."

"Fuck you, Ren!" Steve spat. Like Ren, his dirty blonde hair was long and tied back in a ponytail. His stocky body was nearly vibrating with excitement, and his faded blue eyes were darting back and forth nervously. Charlotte suspected that he was high on something as he turned and shoved Darlene towards Rita and Helen. The three women huddled together as the second man paced back and forth in front of the door.

"Jesus Christ." He moaned. He had a blue bandana on his head and he swiped it off, revealing his bald and gleaming skull, and wiped the sweat from his face with it.

"We're dead, man. We're so fucking dead."

"We're fine, Jasper." Steve grunted.

"Are you kidding me?" Jasper was the smallest of the three. Short and thin, his jeans hanging from his non-existent ass and his leather vest wrapped loosely around his chest, he looked like he was going to vomit. "You shot a goddamn cop! Ren's right – we're going to fry for this."

Steve slammed his fist down on the reception desk. "It's not like I had much choice. Stupid fucking pig practically fell on to our deal."

Ren moved the shade and peered out. "We have to go. Staying here is dangerous."

"Where the hell are we gonna go?" Steve nearly shouted at him.

"We grab our bikes and ride." Ren hissed at him. "For Christ's sake, three different people watched us chase that bleeding cop into here. This place is going to be crawling with cops at any moment."

As if his words summoned them, the faint sound of sirens could be heard.

"Shit!" Ren dropped the shade and stared around the salon. His gaze fell on Jasper. "Go check the back door, make sure it's locked."

Jasper nodded and disappeared into the back of the salon as Charlotte took Vince's hand in her own.

Ren knelt beside her once more and pulled the belt free from Vince's pants. He slid it under Vince, the man groaned with pain, and pushed Charlotte's hand out of the way before adding more towels to the blood-soaked ones. He buckled the belt so that it held the towels firmly against Vince's bleeding side.

Charlotte leaned over him. "Vince? Can you hear me? Squeeze my hand."

Vince squeezed her hand with surprising strength and Charlotte felt a thin thread of relief. "How are you feeling?"

"Like I've been shot." He mumbled.

She smiled and ran her hand over his forehead, leaving a bloody smear, as Ren stood and moved away. "You're going to be just fine. I'll get us both out of this, okay?"

He shook his head. "Just stay quiet and do exactly what they tell you, Charlotte. They'll kill you if you don't." He whispered.

She squeezed his hand. "I'm not afraid. And I don't want you to be afraid either."

She let out a gasp of pain as a hand was twisted into her long, blonde hair and she was yanked to her feet. Steve pulled her head back and she wrinkled her nose in disgust as his stale, tobacco-infused breath washed over her.

"What the fuck are you saying to that pig?"

"I was just telling him he would be fine." She gritted out as he pulled her hair tighter.

"You're a pretty little thing ain't ya?" Steve suddenly crooned. He rubbed his finger across her cheek.

For the first time in three months an emotion broke through the blank numbness that had enveloped her like a thick blanket. She was afraid for Vince. She didn't want Mel to lose him like she had lost Rick. The thought of her own imminent death brought on that same feeling of relief from before, and she had a moment to understand just how broken she really was before Ren was standing in front of them.

"Let her go."

"Since when did you care about some skinny little bitch?" Steve said with an edge to his voice.

"Let her go." Ren repeated himself as the sirens outside grew louder.

"You gonna make me?" Steve sneered.

"If I have to." Ren replied quietly.

Charlotte watched as Ren's eyes grew darker. After a long tense minute, Steve snorted and thrust her towards Ren so roughly, she would have fallen if he hadn't caught her.

He held her against his large body, one hard arm wrapped around her waist and his big hand resting on her hip, as the sirens stopped abruptly.

"They're here." He pulled Charlotte towards the window and carefully peered behind the shade. He swore violently and stared at Steve as Jasper burst back into the salon.

"The back door is locked. But there are cops in the alley."

"There are three cars out front. We've lost our chance." Ren glared at Steve.

"We've got a dying cop and four other hostages. They'll do whatever we ask them to do." Steve answered.

"Jesus, Steve! Are you even listening to yourself?" Ren snarled. "We are in serious trouble here. You need to – "

Steve suddenly pointed his gun at him, and Charlotte felt Ren stiffen before he eased her small body behind his. "Don't be an asshole, Steve."

"No, don't *you* be an asshole, Ren." Steve wiped his nose and glared at him. "Who the fuck is in charge here? Huh? Is it you? Because I certainly don't remember giving up my rightful place as the leader."

Ren, one hand still holding Charlotte firmly, said quietly, "You're in charge, Steve. I'm just trying to be helpful."

"Keep your fucking mouth shut then!" Steve retorted.

"Steve man, we gotta do something." Jasper whined nervously.

"Shut up!" Steve shouted. The shrill ring of the telephone made him jump and he turned towards it.

"That'll be the police." Ren said quietly. "You need to answer it, Steve."

Steve took a deep breath and glanced around the salon. "Everyone just stay the fuck quiet." He reached for the phone.

* * *

Charlotte tucked another cape around Vince's body before checking that her sweater was still supporting his head. She squeezed his shoulder. "How are you doing, Vince?"

"Fine." His face was pale but his voice was strong enough, and she took a deep breath before smiling at him.

"We'll get you to the hospital soon. Mel will be there waiting for you."

"Yeah." He cleared his throat and winced. "I love her so much, Charlotte."

"I know you do, honey. She loves you too."

He squinted up at her. "How are you doing?"

"I'm fine. Don't worry about me." She said firmly. She glanced behind her at Steve who was sniffing a line of fine white powder from the top of the smooth reception desk. "If he keeps snorting that shit up his nose, I'll be able to just walk up and take the guns from him."

Vince frowned. "Don't do anything stupid, Charlotte. These guys are dangerous."

She glanced at Jasper who was sitting on the floor beside Rita's station, and then at Ren who was leaning against the far wall. His arms were folded over his chest and he was staring silently at them.

"Do you know the tall one?" She asked Vince quietly.

He shook his head immediately. "No."

Her brow furrowed a bit. "Are you sure?"

"I'm positive." He said firmly. He turned his head and gave Ren his own quick look. "He seems the most stable of the three of them though."

"Yeah." She whispered. "Of course, that's not saying much is it? Are they part of the motorcycle gang that you were talking about earlier?"

Vince nodded and then coughed weakly, wincing again. Charlotte frowned. For being shot in the side Vince was doing remarkably well, but he needed to be taken to a hospital. She started to stand and Vince took a ragged breath.

"Where are you going?"

"I'll be right back." She squeezed his hand again before standing and walking towards Ren. He didn't move and although he appeared to be relaxed, she sensed the tense energy in his lean body hovering just below the surface.

"He needs to go to the hospital." She said quietly.

When he didn't reply, she frowned at him. "He is going to die. Do you understand that? Or have you snorted too much coke like your idiot friend?"

"Be quiet, girl."

"Your friend is going to get us all killed." She said quietly. "It's been nearly five hours and he has no idea what he's doing. You heard him talking to the hostage negotiator. He's useless."

When he continued to stay silent, she stepped a little closer. "You seem like a smart guy and maybe your brain hasn't been completely addled by the drugs yet. Why are you letting him run things? Are you that weak? That afraid of him?"

He surprised her by suddenly grinning, revealing even white teeth. "Maybe you should be a hostage negotiator. It's a fine technique you know – trying to use our ego's to turn us against each other."

She flushed. "I'm just asking you a simple question. Maybe you should – "

His eyes widened a fraction of a second before Steve had grabbed her hair again and shoved her to her knees. He put the barrel of his gun in the middle of her forehead.

"Did I give you permission to speak to my boy?" He asked softly. He cocked his gun as Darlene made a small moan of dismay and Rita and Helen began to sob quietly.

Charlotte, feeling the cold muzzle of the gun digging into her forehead, stared up at the dirty, blonde man. His eyes were wild and he sniffed continually as he pushed the gun against her forehead.

"Beg me for your life, you stupid little bitch." He whispered.

She realized with sudden clarity that he was about to kill her, and she was helpless to stop the small smile of relief from crossing her face. She closed her eyes and waited for the darkness.

"Stop it, Steve." Ren's deep voice washed over her and she felt the muzzle of the gun waver from her skin as Steve looked at him.

"Christ, this bitch wants to die. You can see it in her eyes." Steve gave a high yodelling laugh.

"Get away from her." Ren's voice was deceptively soft as he pushed his body away from the wall.

"Why are you so fond of this skinny little whore?" Steve grabbed Charlotte's arm and yanked her to her feet. He dragged her to the other women and pushed her down beside them.

Rita buried her face in her shoulder and Charlotte wrapped her arms around the woman as Steve stared down at them.   `

He looked at Jasper and then at Ren, a slow grin creeping on to his face. "Let's play a game."

Jasper, who was leaning over the desk and taking his own snort of white powder, straightened and scrubbed his hand across his nose. "What kind of game?"

Charlotte could see Ren tensing behind Steve as the smaller man grinned lecherously at her. "The kind that will have this cold little bitch all fired up."

"Don't be ridiculous, Steve." Ren growled. "This is neither the time nor the place."

"It never is. Is it, Ren?" Steve snapped. "How many women have I paraded in front of you and you ain't fucked one of them."

"I don't need you choosing a woman for me."

Steve shook his head and stepped closer to Charlotte, sliding the muzzle of his gun through her thick, blonde hair. "Maybe you like boys."

When Ren refused to be goaded by him, Steve squatted down and smiled at Charlotte. "What's your name, bitch?"

"Charlotte." She muttered.

"Pretty name for a pretty girl." He ran his dirty finger across her mouth. "Do you know that I took this asshole in? Gave him shelter, food, allowed him into my gang, and shared freely with him everything that I worked so hard to acquire."

He smiled gently at her. "I've offered him woman after woman – all of them prettier than you – and he's turned each of them down. He insults my generosity by acting like he's too good to fuck one of my women. What do you think of a man who refuses to accept such a generous gift from the man who has given him so much?"

When she remained quiet, he yanked on her hair. "Answer me!"

"I think he's a fool."

He laughed. "Oh, I do like you." He glanced behind him at Ren. "And I think he likes you too."

He stood and turned to Ren. "Tell you what, old friend. I'm going to give you one last chance to prove your loyalty to me."

He waved his gun at Charlotte. "Stand up, bitch."

She untangled herself from Rita's grip and stood, walking forward when Steve motioned the gun at her.

"You're going to fuck her."

Ren stiffened. "No I'm not."

Steve shrugged. "Fine, then I'll kill her."

He raised the gun and pointed it at Charlotte.

"Don't be a goddamn idiot, Steve. You're so fucking high right now you don't know what the hell you're doing."

Ren snarled. "What do you think all those cops out there will do if they hear a gunshot? You start killing hostages and we're finished."

Steve laughed. "I've still got four more hostages, Ren. They hear a gunshot and all they'll do is phone again and try and talk me into giving myself up."

"What do you think, Charlotte?" Steve smiled at her. "He ain't a bad lookin' man. One quick fuck - or death. Make your choice."

She stared silently at him and Steve laughed again. "This bitch is crazy! Jasper, you ever seen a bitch want to die so bad in your life?"

Jasper shook his head no as Steve turned back to Ren. "What'll it be? You going to have this woman's death on your conscience?"

Ren shrugged and tried to sound nonchalant. "You said it yourself. The woman wants to die."

"Now you're both just bein' difficult." Steve said sullenly.

"I'm not playing your game, Steve." Ren said quietly.

"Oh you'll play. And so will she." Steve suddenly pointed the gun at Vince. "The rules are changing. You fuck her, or hell any of these bitches, to prove your loyalty to me or I'll kill the cop."

Charlotte inhaled sharply and Steve grinned at her. "That got you, didn't it?"

He winked at Ren. "Ready to play now, Ren?"

Ren shrugged again. "What the hell do I care about the life of some cop? Go ahead and kill him."

"Suit yourself." Steve started to stride towards Vince.

"Wait! I'll play the game." Charlotte's voice rang out loudly and Steve stopped.

"Christ, she's practically begging you for it now, Ren." Steve yodelled laughter again. He waved the gun at Charlotte and she walked over and stood next to Ren.

Vince struggled to sit up, before falling back to the floor and panting harshly. "Charlotte, don't do this. I'd rather die."

"Be quiet, Vince." Charlotte snapped.

"Play the game, Ren." Steve said softly. "Prove your loyalty and I'll let the cop and your new little fuck buddy live. Go on now."

Ren stared down at Charlotte, his eyes dark and unreadable, before suddenly taking her hand. He started to lead her to the back.

"Where the hell do you think you're going?" Steve shouted.

"To the back." Ren turned and stared at Steve steadily. "I'm not fucking her in front of you."

Steve eyed him shrewdly. "Fine. But if you even think of letting the cops in through the back or letting that bitch go, know that I'll kill the cop and at least one of these other bitches before they take me down. You get what I'm sayin'?"

"I get it." Ren said tightly. He pulled Charlotte past the curtain that separated the back room from the salon.

* * *

Saving Charlotte will be available at
www.amazon.com in January of 2015.

If you would like more information about Elizabeth Kelly, please visit her at:

https://www.facebook.com/elizabethkellybooks
or
http://www.elizabethkellybooks.blogspot.ca/
or
https://twitter.com/ElizabethKBooks

Write to her at:
mailto:elizabethkellybooks@gmail.com

Other books by Elizabeth Kelly:

Tempted
http://www.amazon.com/dp/B00DYAU0YE

Twice Tempted
http://www.amazon.com/dp/B00F3G29QY

Red Moon
http://www.amazon.com/dp/B00ETIRVAG

Red Moon Rising (Red Moon Second Generation Series)
http://www.amazon.com/dp/B00HYEFD70

Dark Moon (Red Moon Second Generation Series)
http://www.amazon.com/dp/B00JQRQE5I

Alpha Moon (Red Moon Second Generation Series)
http://www.amazon.com/dp/B00MP2P1XW

The Necessary Engagement
http://www.amazon.com/dp/B00FBSEALQ

Amelia's Touch
http://www.amazon.com/dp/B00G1IL1OY

The Rancher's Daughter
http://www.amazon.com/dp/B00GO3HQE0

Healing Gabriel
http://www.amazon.com/dp/B00HRGN8ZY

The Recruit (Book One)
http://www.amazon.com/dp/B00IJNOUA6

The Recruit (Book Two)
http://www.amazon.com/dp/B00LVHZ1KK

The Contract
http://www.amazon.com/dp/B00K514II4

37255115R00158

Made in the USA
Charleston, SC
02 January 2015